Sticking Up for Sophia

"Liz, are you telling us that the school play, the most important event of the whole school year, is in the hands of raggedy Sophia Rizzo?" Jessica gave an anguished cry.

"Sophia and five other kids, including your own sister," Elizabeth said. "Besides, if you'd been with me this afternoon, you'd know what a terrific writer Sophia is!"

"If I'd been with you this afternoon," said Jessica, "I'd probably have been sick. I can't believe you set foot in that girl's house."

"Yeah," Steven agreed. "Who needs to hang out with losers like that?"

In an instant Elizabeth's happiness about the show was destroyed. She looked at her brother and sister, finding it hard to believe that her own family could be so shallow and heartless. "How do you know what Sophia's house is like if you've never been there?" she asked them. "And how do you know what she's like if you've never even talked to her? And whoever left that cruel note in Sophia's desk doesn't know the first thing about giving people a fair shake."

"Liz," Jessica said, "it's not as if I wrote that note all by myself. The Unicorns took a vote on it, and we all agreed this town would be a lot better off without the Rizzo family."

Elizabeth was tired and angry. She was disappointed in Jessica and Steven. "If being friends with Sophia means being left out by snobs like the Unicorns, then I won't mind in the least!"

Bantam-Skylark Books in the SWEET VALLEY TWINS series
Ask your bookseller for the books you have missed

SWEET VALLEY TWINS

Against
the Rules

Written by
Jamie Suzanne

Created by
FRANCINE PASCAL

A BANTAM SKYLARK BOOK®
TORONTO · NEW YORK · LONDON · SYDNEY · AUCKLAND

AGAINST THE RULES

A Bantam Skylark Book / June 1987

Skylark Books is a registered trademark of Bantam Books, Inc. Registered in U.S. Patent and Trademark Office and elsewhere.

Sweet Valley High and Sweet Valley Twins are trademarks of Francine Pascal.

Conceived by Francine Pascal.

Cover art by James Mathewuse.

ISBN 0-553-15518-0

Published simultaneously in the United States and Canada

Bantam Books are published by Bantam Books, Inc. Its trademark, consisting of the words "Bantam Books" and the portrayal of a rooster, is Registered in U.S. Patent and Trademark Office and in other countries. Marca Registrada. Bantam Books, Inc., 666 Fifth Avenue, New York, New York 10103.

PRINTED IN THE UNITED STATES OF AMERICA

O   0 9 8 7 6 5 4

Against
the Rules

One

◇

"Sophia Rizzo!" Jessica Wakefield's mouth puckered as if she had just tasted a lemon. "You mean you're walking home with the biggest creep in Sweet Valley Middle School?" She stopped in her tracks and stared at her sister. "If you weren't my identical twin, Elizabeth, I'd say you had lost your marbles!"

"We may be identical twins, Jess," Elizabeth answered, "but we sure don't think alike, especially on the subject of Sophia."

Elizabeth was right. Although the two Wakefield girls looked like mirror images of each other, they seldom agreed on friends. Jessica liked to discuss the newest fashions and gossip about boys, and she chose friends who were as pretty and popular as she was. Elizabeth, on the other hand, loved people, particularly talented, imaginative ones like their dark-eyed classmate.

Jessica turned on her heel indignantly, her sun-streaked ponytail bouncing. "Suit yourself. I've got Booster practice anyway. But, I'm warning you, Liz, if you keep picking up strays, one of these days you're going to get bitten!"

Elizabeth laughed. She was used to her twin's strong opinions, but she was also used to going her own way. Even though the whole school seemed to dislike Sophia and her family, Elizabeth had taken the time to get to know the petite sixth grader. Only a few weeks before, Sophia had begun writing articles for *The Sweet Valley Sixers*, the class newspaper Elizabeth organized. What a surprise Sophia's first articles had been. They were the funniest, best-written stories that had been turned in all year!

"If Sophia Rizzo bites me, I hope I catch her way with words." Let everyone else make fun of the Rizzos' old house and whisper about Sophia's "bad" brother. Elizabeth was getting to know her new reporter better every day. And she was getting to like her more and more.

"I just don't see why you have to spend time with a social reject," Jessica persisted. "I mean her brother is a criminal."

Elizabeth had heard that Anthony Rizzo had stolen a VCR from someone's house and had been sent to reform school. But what did that have to do with Sophia? "If her brother made some mistakes, does that make Sophia a criminal, too?" Elizabeth asked.

"It makes her off-limits for anyone who cares about her image." Jessica was always worried about what other people, especially "important" people, thought.

"Well, Sophia is turning into the best reporter on our paper. To me, that's more important than a lot of silly gossip." Elizabeth looked at her watch. "I'd better get going. I told Sophia I'd meet her after school so we can squeeze some news about the play out of Mr. Bowman. This could be our lead story, and I want Sophia to help write it."

Suddenly Jessica looked interested. "That's right!" she exclaimed. Like many of the students at Sweet Valley Middle School, Jessica had been anxious for the English teacher to announce the name of the play that would be the school's biggest production. Jessica, who loved performing, was counting on a leading role. "I can't wait to try out. I hope he picks a really splashy musical, with lots of singing and dancing."

"When the news breaks, Jess," Elizabeth promised her sister, "you'll be the first to know. OK?"

"You bet. Oh, Liz, since you're not doing anything important, would you take these books with you? I just know the squad is going to want to stop in at the Dairi Burger after practice."

Before Elizabeth could tell her twin that working on the *Sixers* was at least as important as munching fries and drinking shakes with her friends, Jessica had dumped three text books and a fat spiral notebook into her arms, with a, "See you at home, big sister!"

Elizabeth stood on the wide front steps of the school and watched her twin race off to practice. Even though the two of them joked about Jessica's being four minutes younger, sometimes Elizabeth really did feel like an older sister to her headstrong identical twin.

Sophia, small and dark, joined Elizabeth at the

top of the stairs. "I thought maybe you'd forgotten our meeting, so I came looking for you," she said. "Here, let me help you with those books. It looks like you're doing homework for two."

Grateful, Elizabeth let her new friend take some of the books, and together they headed back into the sprawling brick school. "I may not be doing homework for two," she told Sophia, "but I sure am *carrying* it for two. I guess Jessica doesn't want the crowd at the Dairi Burger to think she's a bookworm."

At the mention of Jessica, Sophia's face took on a faraway look. "Gee," she admitted, "I only wish I had half the friends your sister does! She's always so busy. Just like you, Elizabeth."

Not exactly like me, thought Elizabeth to herself. If she were Jessica she'd have turned the other way as soon as she spotted Sophia Rizzo. "I don't think either of us is missing anything by not being with the 'snob squad' at the Dairi Burger, Sophia." She smiled. "It's funny. I like most of the girls who'll be there. But somehow when they all get together, they're not as nice as when you talk to them alone."

"I know what you mean," Sophia agreed.

The two girls stood wordlessly in the hall, and Sophia seemed to be trying to decide something. Finally, she reached into the pocket of her faded skirt and pulled out a rumpled square of paper. With an expression of shame and embarrassment, she handed it to Elizabeth. "I found this in my desk this morning."

Elizabeth's blue-green eyes filled with anger as she read what had been scribbled on the sheet. "We don't need your kind in Sweet Valley," the note read. "Get out, and take your brother with you." At the bottom of the note was a clumsily drawn horse with a big horn in the center of its head.

"The Unicorns! How could they?!" Elizabeth rolled the paper into a tight ball between her fingers. "I knew they were silly gossips, but I never thought they'd go this far." The Unicorns was an exclusive club that included most members of the Booster squad, the best dressers, and the snobbiest girls in the middle school. The girls in the group were supposed to be as beautiful and special as the magical beast after which they'd named their club. At the beginning of sixth grade, Jessica Wakefield had joined and found that she fit right in with The Unicorns. It took only one meeting for Elizabeth to decide the group was not for her.

As she studied Sophia's stricken face, Elizabeth decided it was time she had a long talk with Jessica. People had been persecuting Sophia because of her brother's mistakes long enough. It had started when Anthony Rizzo was sent to a reform school, and now that he was back in Sweet Valley, things seemed to be getting worse. "I'm so sorry, Sophia," Elizabeth said, touching her friend's shoulder gently. "They don't even know your brother."

Sophia's eyes were filling up. "That's just what Mama says. She says she doesn't know her own son since Papa left us. Tony doesn't listen to her anymore. He doesn't listen to anyone."

Elizabeth felt terrible. She thought of her own older brother, Steven, and couldn't picture life at home without his constant teasing and awful jokes. "Hey," she reminded Sophia, "we've got work to do. Remember?"

Slowly, Sophia returned the note to her pocket. For a minute, she seemed to struggle with tears, but at last she smiled back at Elizabeth, her brown eyes warm and proud. "That's right. I hope we can convince Mr. Bowman to tell us his choice for the play—if he's made up his mind, that is."

"What do you mean?" Elizabeth asked. "Rehearsals are supposed to begin this month."

"I know, but he told our English class that the play might start late this year. He said it would be a real surprise for everyone."

"Everyone except the hardworking staff of the *Sixers*," announced a voice behind them. Turning, the girls were surprised to see Mr. Bowman with a stack of papers under one arm. Elizabeth couldn't help noticing with a secret giggle that his paisley tie clashed with his checked shirt. She often wondered how anyone so nice could come up with such awful clothing combinations.

"I was on my way to the office to run off a test," Mr. Bowman continued. "And, if you'd care to join me, I've got a real scoop for you two."

Elizabeth and Sophia exchanged glances. It was as if Mr. Bowman had read their minds. Now on the trail of their big story, they followed him down the tiled hall, asking him question after question.

"Is it going to be a musical, Mr. Bowman?"
"Will you give major roles to sixth graders?"
"When will the auditions be?"
"Who's the author?"

When they reached the office, Mr. Bowman opened the door, then held up one hand, laughing. "Whoa, now. Just a minute! Let me answer one question at a time. And," he added, winking, "let's start with the last one."

The girls drew close to the old ditto machine as their teacher prepared the first master for printing. "I think you should know," he said as he turned the crank, "that we're not going to use a famous author this year. This play will be the first thing they've written."

"They?" Both Elizabeth and Sophia looked puzzled.

"Maybe I should say *you*," Mr. Bowman corrected himself.

Two mouths dropped open, and four eyes popped with excitement.

"Yes, you. I've decided to let the students write their own play this year, and the department has picked a writing committee composed of the two best English students from each grade in the school. Guess who the two sixth-grade representatives are?"

The girls could hardly believe their ears. First they hugged each other, and then they gasped. "Do you really think we can do it?" Elizabeth asked.

"Of course you can," Mr. Bowman assured her. "There's enough talent on the writing team we've chosen that I expect nothing less than a smash hit from the six of you!"

Sophia beamed. She looked happier than Elizabeth could ever remember seeing her. "Oh, Mr. Bowman, when do we start? I've got so many ideas, I want to write them all down before I lose them!"

The teacher laughed again. "Well, there's no time like the present. I'll give you the names of the team members, and you can call them and arrange your first meeting." He handed her a sheet with the names and phone numbers of the committee neatly typed in two columns.

"Will you be our adviser, Mr. Bowman?" Elizabeth knew how much guidance he had given the *Sixers'* staff, and she was sure the play committee could use the same helping hand.

"I'd be honored." Mr. Bowman bent his long body in a formal bow while the old ditto machine clattered away. "Now, don't you two have a story to write?"

A few minutes later, Elizabeth and Sophia were huddled at two desks in the empty study hall. Soon they had finished their lead story. The following afternoon, when the final copies of *The Sweet Valley Sixers* were mimeographed and distributed, everyone in school would know. "I can hardly believe it," Elizabeth told Sophia.

"The best part of all," Sophia reminded her, "is the play itself. Just think, this play means we get to tell our own story instead of acting out someone else's!"

"Hey!" Elizabeth grabbed her pencil. "That makes a perfect headline for our big news. 'Student Play to Feature Students' Own Story,' by Sophia Rizzo and Elizabeth Wakefield. What do you think?"

"Can't we leave my name off, Elizabeth?"

Elizabeth couldn't understand. "But, Sophia," she protested, "you've written as much of this story as I have. You've asked me to leave your name off every article you've written for the *Sixers* so far, but this is our biggest news yet. I don't want to take all the credit."

A shadow seemed to cover Sophia's face, erasing the excitement it had shown just a minute before. "I—I don't think so," she said. "I don't think anyone would want to read a story with my name on it." Her shaky voice and downcast eyes made Elizabeth remember the ugly note from The Unicorns. "The name Rizzo doesn't exactly make anybody around here stand up and cheer."

"And it won't either, if you keep letting them make you afraid!" Elizabeth exclaimed. "Look, this story was written by both of us, and if anyone has any complaints, they'll have to make them to both of us." She held out her hand, and slowly Sophia took it. "We're friends aren't we?"

"Friends?" The word that Elizabeth had used so easily sounded like magic when Sophia said it. "Friends. I guess we are!" Lit up by a huge smile, her face looked twice as pretty as usual.

Immediately Sophia seemed more confident and outgoing. "Would you like to walk home to my house and call the committee from there?" she asked, grabbing her sweater and gathering her books. "I've been writing plays for Tony and me ever since we were little. I'd love to show you some of them."

No one Elizabeth knew had ever visited the Rizzos' small house near the Patmans' canning factory. Elizabeth thought of all the rumors she'd heard about Anthony Rizzo, Sophia's brother, all the talk about how he had turned bad after their father left them; how he should have gone to prison instead of reform school; how he'd never amount to anything. Then she remembered the note from The Unicorns and the hurt in Sophia's eyes. It was time someone got to the bottom of things and put an end to all the gossip. Smiling and hoping Sophia couldn't see how uncertain she felt, Elizabeth picked up her books and joined her friend. "I'd be glad to come home with you," she said. "And I'd love to read your plays."

Two

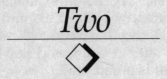

Sophia's mother greeted the two girls at the Rizzos' tiny house. She was small and dark like her daughter, and, like Sophia, her clothes were faded from age and countless washings.

Mrs. Rizzo shook Elizabeth's hand and waved her into the living room. Even though the outside of the house had paint peeling away and shutters that hung away from the windows, the inside was cozy and well-cared for. The furnishings were simple, but each piece was covered with bright, hand-crocheted pillows and afghans. Carefully tended plants brightened the room.

Mrs. Rizzo spoke with a heavy Italian accent. Elizabeth noticed that she moved very slowly and limped when she walked into the kitchen to get the girls drinks. But she seemed almost as excited and happy as Sophia herself when she heard about the school play. "That's so wonderful!" she said, clapping her hands like a child.

After Sophia and Elizabeth called everyone on the list and set up the first meeting of the play committee, they went to Sophia's room. From the drawer of a small dresser by her bed, Sophia pulled out a stack of papers and several bulging notebooks. "I've never showed these to anyone before," she told Elizabeth shyly. "Except of course Mama and Tony."

They sat on Sophia's faded, flowered bedspread, and Elizabeth opened one of the notebooks. It was filled with short plays and sketches, some written in a childish scrawl, others in more grown-up script.

"I guess I started writing as soon as I could pick up a pencil," Sophia said apologetically as Elizabeth paged through some of the poems, stories, and plays. The early plays had only two parts, usually a beautiful princess and a troll or wizard. All the trolls' and wizards' lines had big *T*'s, for Tony, written in front of them, and all the princesses' speeches were preceded by *S*'s, for Sophia.

"You notice I always typecast?" Sophia winked mischievously. "I guess that's why Tony started calling me Princess."

Elizabeth could hardly believe Sophia was speaking so fondly of the boy everyone said such horrible things about. As she read over some of the skits, she couldn't help laughing. Even the early ones had a funny, sweet quality that kept her reading from one page to the next. As she read, she tried to imagine Sophia's brother helping his sister stage the stories for their mother. It was like trying to imagine Jesse James starring as Peter Pan!

"Where *is* your brother?" Elizabeth asked nervously.

"He's in school. Should be home any minute."

Suddenly, Elizabeth felt she should leave. She had met Tony Rizzo once before, when he'd come to pick Sophia up from school, and she didn't like him.

"Well, I'd really better get home now. I'll see you at school tomorrow. Maybe you and I could run off the *Sixers* and hand them out after school."

"I'd like to, Elizabeth." Sophia looked worried. "But I promised Mama I'd help her shop." She looked down at her hands. "You see, we don't have a car, and Mama can't get around too easily. When she had a job at the factory, people at work used to give her rides home or to the store." She raised her head and studied Elizabeth's clear blue-green eyes. "But her leg got worse, and she had to stop work. Now there's just me and Tony to help her. And Tony— Well, he's not the same as when we were little. He doesn't seem to care anymore."

"Never mind," Elizabeth said, wishing she hadn't asked. "I can get somebody else on the staff to help me." She handed Sophia the stack of plays and smiled gently. "These are good, Sophia. *Really* good. I especially like the one about the girl who feels jealous of her little sister. I've heard a lot of kids in our class complain about how the babies in their families always get more attention."

"I guess I've outgrown fairy tales," admitted Sophia. "I used to love adventure and romance, but now I like to write about things that happen to real people."

"But you don't even have a baby sister."

Sophia smiled. "I don't need to. All I need to do is understand how one would make me feel."

"Well, you sure are terrific at putting yourself in other peoples' places." Elizabeth thought for a moment. "Hey, do anything you have to do after school tomorrow, but don't you *dare* miss our committee meeting on Wednesday. We need you!"

Elizabeth thanked Mrs. Rizzo, then hurried out the door and headed home. Elizabeth knew that what she'd told Sophia was true. The committee really did need her special gifts. In fact, this year's play might very well be the best ever because of the way Sophia could crawl into peoples' heads and know just what they were thinking.

As her path took her back into her own familiar neighborhood, filled with spacious homes on carefully manicured lawns, Elizabeth wished that more people shared Sophia's talent for understanding others. But, as Jessica came bounding out of the Wakefields' front door, Elizabeth wondered if the happy, pampered kids of Sweet Valley would ever be able to put themselves in Sophia's place.

"Wait till you hear!" Jessica's smile was so broad it showed the dimple in her left cheek. "It's too good to believe!"

"Try me." Elizabeth couldn't help smiling, even though she had no idea what Jessica was so excited about.

"We're going to L.A. next month! Dad's biggest clients want company for their daughter on a weekend trip." Mr. Wakefield was a lawyer in Sweet Valley, and the family was used to entertaining his firm's clients. "We'll go shopping, stay at a big hotel, and best of all—we'll see *Shout*. Isn't it too perfect?" Jessica jumped up and down as she led her sister into the Wakefields' sunny, Spanish-tiled kitchen.

Their mother was already home from her part-time job as an interior designer. "It's true," she told Elizabeth with a wink. "Your father called me at work today. It seems you two are headed for an overnight trip to the big city!"

Elizabeth, almost as excited as her twin, dropped her pile of books on the table and raced to join her mother by the sink. Even though she didn't think there was any spot on earth so perfect as Sweet Valley, with its forever blue skies and sparkling white beach, Elizabeth couldn't help being thrilled at the prospect of a trip to Los Angeles. "Wow! Maybe we can eat at that great Mexican restaurant on Sunset Strip," she exclaimed.

"And tour a Hollywood studio," suggested Jessica, hugging her twin.

"And visit Chinatown!"

"And Beverly Hills!"

Mrs. Wakefield stopped rinsing dishes and put up one hand. "Whoa! We're talking about two days, not a week!" Blond and slim, the twins' mother looked like a grown-up version of her daughters. Now her pretty, tanned face broke into an amused smile. "I don't think the Martins have quite enough time or energy for everything you've got planned."

"At least we'll get to see *Shout*." Jessica, who

kept a life-size poster of the popular musical's dancers over her bed, couldn't wait to see the show. She counted the time before their trip on her fingers. "It's nearly six weeks till we leave! I'll never last. I just know I'll die of excitement first!" Her enthusiasm seemed to light up the room. "I know every one of the songs by heart. And I've made up some great dances to go with the record." With that, she grabbed her mother by the waist and gracefully whirled her around the kitchen.

Elizabeth couldn't resist joining them, and soon all three were twirling across the floor. Laughing as hard as her daughters, Mrs. Wakefield scattered drops of water behind her as she danced.

"Hey, time out," she protested at last. "If I don't get these dishes rinsed and in the washer, I won't be able to pick up Steven from basketball practice." She glanced anxiously at her watch. "Unless, of course, I've got two volunteers who'll finish the job for me."

Jessica's smile vanished, replaced by a tragic expression that would have been appropriate for a lost orphan. "Mom, I wish I *could* help. But Ms. Wyler gave our class enough math homework to keep me busy from now until midnight! I guess she thinks we're all math whizzes like Elizabeth."

Elizabeth grinned. "I think I know just where that compliment is leading, little sister." She stepped beside her mother and took a plate from the water. "Go ahead, Mom. You can pick up Steven while I finish here. I only wish Jessica had time to stay and hear about the play." She stacked the plate in the washer, then glanced over her shoulder at her twin.

"I'll bet if she didn't have so much homework she'd be thrilled to learn she knows the authors personally."

"What?" Jessica exclaimed. "You mean Mr. Bowman's chosen our show? Oh, Liz, maybe I could put off my math for just a minute or two."

Elizabeth smiled mischievously. "Long enough to help me with these dishes?"

Their mother laughed and headed for the garage. "Thank you *both*," she told them. "I'll be back with reinforcements in a minute."

"If she means Steven," Jessica said grimly as she took a plate from her twin, "we'll have to wait more than a minute before *he* helps with the dishes!"

Elizabeth bent her head, scrubbing the bottom of a frying pan. "How can you say that about our considerate older brother? Why, I'm certain he helped rinse the dishes last Thanksgiving."

"Come to think of it," added Jessica, "you're right. That was the last time he cleaned his room, too!"

"Not true!" announced the tall, brown-haired boy who stepped suddenly through the back door.

"Steven!" The twins exclaimed in surprise.

"Some people," growled Steven, looking pointedly at Jessica, "shouldn't talk about neat rooms, especially people who try on their whole wardrobe every day before school."

Jessica ignored her brother's teasing remark and dried her hands on a dish towel. "I thought you were at basketball practice. Mom just went to pick you up."

Steven ambled toward the refrigerator, opened

the door, and stared at the food inside. "I got a ride home. Hope Mom's not sore." After loading a plate with three slices of bread, Swiss cheese, ham, two tomatoes, and a dill pickle, he closed the refrigerator door and sat at the kitchen table.

"It's amazing," noted Jessica, sitting beside him. "Practically a scientific miracle. The way you stuff yourself you should weigh three hundred pounds!"

Trim and athletic, Steven grinned at her. "I do. It's all in my brain."

"Your fat head, you mean."

"Hey, you two," Elizabeth reminded them. "While you're arguing, I'm the only one finishing the dishes!"

"Sorry, big sister, but Mr. Big Deal High School Freshman never does his share." Jessica remained seated, pouting dramatically while her brother started constructing his triple-decker sandwich. "Besides, Liz, you didn't tell me about the play."

"Ah, yes," interrupted Steven. "I remember when *I* was an immature middle school student. We put on the best play in the history of the school. So, whatever show you've picked," he announced between bites, "it'll never be as great as the job we did."

"The only great thing about the show you were in," said Jessica, "was that you had a small part."

"We aren't *picking* a show this year," Elizabeth told them proudly. "We're *writing* one ourselves!"

"What do you mean?" Jessica looked shocked. "Aren't we doing a musical?"

"That depends on what the committee decides." Elizabeth couldn't hide her excitement any longer.

Earlier, the prospect of a trip to Los Angeles had made her forget her own big news. But now, her face glowing, she told her sister and brother about Mr. Bowman's decision to let the students write their own play. She told them how he'd chosen two students from each grade to develop the show. Finally, she described her visit to Sophia's house and the wonderful plays her talented friend had written.

"Liz, are you telling us that the most important event of the whole school year is in the hands of raggedy Rizzo?" Jessica gave an anguished cry.

"Sophia *and* five other kids, including your own sister. Besides, if you'd been with me this afternoon, you'd know what a terrific writer Sophia is!"

"If I'd been with you this afternoon," said Jessica, wrinkling her nose in disgust, "I'd probably have been sick. Honestly, Liz, I can't believe you set foot in that girl's house."

"Yeah," agreed Steven. "I'd sure think twice before *I* visited that neighborhood. Who needs to hang out with losers like that?"

In an instant Elizabeth's happiness about the show was destroyed. She looked at her brother and sister, finding it hard to believe that her own family could be so shallow and heartless. "How do you know what Sophia's house is like if you've never *been* there?" she asked them. "And how do you know what *she's* like if you've never even talked to her?"

"I may not know Sophia," Steven told her, "but I sure know her brother. Well enough to stay as far away from him as I can."

"Just how do you get to know somebody by staying away from him, big brother?"

"It's not just talk, Elizabeth." Steven looked suddenly serious and grown-up. "Anthony Rizzo is trouble. He's stolen everything from TV's to cars. And my bet is, he hasn't cleaned up his act, even after reform school."

"And to think his sister is helping to write *my* school play!" Jessica muttered angrily. "It probably won't have a single song in it. It'll probably be all about crime and murder and disgusting bloodshed."

Elizabeth couldn't believe what she was hearing. "Come on, Jess. You know better than that. Or do you?"

"What do you mean, Liz?"

"I mean anyone who could leave that cruel note in Sophia's desk doesn't know the first thing about giving people a fair shake."

"Well, anyone who lives in a run-down house and watches stolen TV doesn't know the first thing about living with decent, normal human beings!" Jessica exclaimed. "Besides, Liz, it's not as if I wrote that note all by myself. The Unicorns took a vote on it, and we all agreed this town would be a lot better off without the Rizzos."

"Well, for once I think Jess's dumb club has the right idea," Steven declared. "I mean you don't know Tony Rizzo. He doesn't care how he dresses or what he says. When he's in school at all, that is. I'll bet he hasn't been to half his classes this year." Steven paused, then leaned toward Elizabeth. "And what do you suppose he's doing on all the days he's absent?"

"Probably taking things that don't belong to him," Jessica guessed before Elizabeth could answer.

"I sure hope you know what you're getting into, Elizabeth." Without finishing his sandwich, Steven stood up and carried his plate to the sink.

"She doesn't care, Steven," said Jessica. "Whenever Lizzie likes someone, she plunges right in without thinking. Why, if she keeps on being friends with the Rizzos, she'll be as much a social outcast as shabby Sophia!"

Elizabeth was tired and angry. She was disappointed in Jessica and Steven, and even more in herself for not being able to persuade them to change their minds. "If being friends with Sophia," she said, loading the last dish and closing the dishwasher, "means being left out by snobs like the Unicorns, then I won't mind in the least."

Three
◇

Tired and discouraged, Elizabeth had just opened the door to her room and gotten a glimpse of her inviting blue bedspread when she heard a familiar voice on the landing.

"Where's my other favorite daughter?"

"Daddy!" Elizabeth raced back down the stairs to give her father a welcome home hug. Mr. Wakefield, his friendly brown eyes set in a handsome tanned face, dropped his briefcase to kiss Elizabeth. "Boy, I'm glad you're home," she told him, feeling now that everything would be set straight.

"I am too. I only wish I were bringing better news with me."

Elizabeth noticed the frown lines by her father's mouth. "What's the matter, Daddy?"

"I think I'd better break this to you and Jessica together." He took Elizabeth by the hand and led her back into the kitchen to join Jessica and Steven.

"What's up?" Jessica looked as puzzled as Elizabeth felt. "Is it about our trip to L.A.?"

"I'm afraid so." Their father sat beside Steven at the table, where he could look at both his daughters. "It seems there's been a misunderstanding about the Martins' invitation."

"Why, Daddy? Can't we go?" asked Jessica.

"Only one of you is invited." Mr. Wakefield clearly felt awful about the news.

Elizabeth and Jessica stared at each other, looking like two reflections of the same disappointed girl. "Which one?"

"Either one. I guess I didn't really understand the situation, and I just assumed both of you could go. But it seems the Martins have a daughter just about your age, and they've only got tickets and accommodations for four."

"You mean one of us has to stay home?" Elizabeth wasn't even surprised. Somehow this disappointment just blended in with the whole awful afternoon. One look at her twin, however, made it clear to her that Jessica wasn't taking things as calmly. Her huge eyes were already filling with tears.

Shout was her favorite show in the world, and this setback was more than she could bear.

"But, Daddy, I simply have to see *Shout*. If I don't, I'll absolutely die!"

"I'm certain it won't come to that," her father assured Jessica. "I only wish your mother and I could buy an extra ticket and send you both. But *Shout*'s been sold out for months."

Elizabeth knew she would have loved the trip to Los Angeles. She was always thrilled when she saw the sky-high buildings along the Miracle Mile. And it was fun to watch so many people in one place at the same time. But she also knew how much her twin had been counting on the show, and she had no doubt about who should go to L.A. "If only one of us can go, Dad," she told her father, "it should be Jessica."

Jessica's face brightened. "Oh, Lizzie! You're the most wonderful sister in the entire universe!"

Mr. Wakefield, however, did not seem relieved. This wasn't the first time Elizabeth had given in to Jessica's strong will. And this time, he was determined things would be different. "No," he told them. "As soon as your mother gets home, we'll draw straws. I want to be absolutely fair about this."

Elizabeth didn't say a word. But as she heard her mother's car pull into the driveway and looked at Jessica's stricken face, she wondered how fair it would be if the twin that had memorized every word of her favorite musical had to miss it.

"Why is it my children always use the phone when they need a ride, but never remember to call when they don't?" Mrs. Wakefield walked into the kitchen with a smile that suggested she wasn't as upset with Steven as she should have been.

"Gosh, Mom, I'm sorry," Steven said with an embarrassed grin. "I got a ride home with Jimmy Lynch, and I guess I kind of forgot to let you know."

His mother tousled Steven's hair and sat beside him at the table. "That's OK. As long as your team keeps playing the way they are, I can't really complain."

"That's right," Ned Wakefield agreed. "If your team wins one more game, I'll be treating everyone to sundaes at Casey's next week."

Steven, who was in the starting lineup for Sweet Valley High's junior varsity basketball team, blushed proudly. "You really didn't think we could do it, did you, Dad? You didn't think we'd go undefeated."

"I bet a lot of sundaes, you wouldn't," his father told him. "Twelve, to be exact!"

"Fifteen, counting the coaches," Steven corrected.

"Seventeen, counting us," insisted Jessica and Elizabeth in unison.

"Do I hear eighteen?" Mr. Wakefield turned to his wife, laugh lines crinkling beside his brown eyes. "My treat."

"I never could resist Casey's double-scoop specials." Mrs. Wakefield laughed and looked fondly at the faces around the table. "I've raised three children on them."

Mr. Wakefield coughed nervously. "Well, I suppose it's time to get down to business," he said uneasily. "I'm afraid there's been a mistake, Alice." He explained the misunderstanding about the twins' trip to Los Angeles. "I thought the fairest thing to do would be to draw straws," he finished.

"I already told Dad that I'd stay home," Elizabeth volunteered. "After all, the trip's not for almost six weeks yet, and I'll be busy working on our play." She was dying to tell her mother the good news, but she knew that it would have to wait. "Or maybe you and I can visit that little antique store that's opened up off Beach Drive." She loved browsing through old, rusty treasures and helping her mother find something that would add the finishing touch to a client's home.

"I'm afraid your dad and I have already committed ourselves that weekend, Elizabeth." Mrs. Wakefield stood up and took a plate from the cupboard over the stove. She piled it with crackers, fruit, and cheese. "That's the day of the Sloans' anniversary. They've invited us to a big boat party, so whoever stays home will be on her own." She returned to the table, placing the snack in the center.

"That's OK," said Elizabeth. "There'll be lots to do."

"I explained to the girls that I wanted each one to have a fair chance to go." Mr. Wakefield reached across the table to take the twins' hands. "That's why I thought the best solution was to draw straws. I've never been sure exactly what the phrase means."

"I've got a good idea," said Steven. "I'll write a number on a piece of paper. Jessica and Elizabeth can both try to guess it, and whoever comes closer wins." He leaned back, and balanced his chair on one leg to reach the kitchen "junk drawer." He pulled out a tablet of paper, tore off a single sheet, and, hiding his work as if it were a secret document, scribbled a number on it.

"But, Daddy," objected Jessica, "what if I lose?" Her long lashes closed over eyes that had filled again with tears. "I've just got to see *Shout*. Please, please. I'll clean up my room every day for the rest of my life!"

"I think your father's right. This is the only way to settle things." Mrs. Wakefield didn't like to see Jessica so miserable, but she wanted to be fair about something so important.

Everyone held his breath as the twins decided on their numbers. Elizabeth almost wished the Martins had never made their offer. She felt a sinking sensation in her heart when Steven announced that the number she'd picked was only one away from the number he'd written down!

Jessica's number was four off and, when she realized she had lost, she began to sob uncontrollably. Through her tears, she stared at her family. Everyone *else* was happy, she thought. Elizabeth had just been chosen to help write the school play, and now she was going to Los Angeles with the Martins. Steven was nearly popping over his basketball team's record. And her parents were going to a boat party for two of their oldest friends. But what about her?

All she had wanted was this trip to Los Angeles. Why, as soon as their mother had told her about it, she'd gotten right on the phone and boasted to her best friend, Lila Fowler, she'd be seeing *Shout*.

"Wow!" Lila had squealed. "You are so lucky, Jessica. Daddy says he's been trying to get us tickets for two months!"

And Jessica had felt like a queen. If George Fowler, one of the wealthiest men in Sweet Valley, couldn't get a ticket, she was in for a real treat.

But now all her hopes were dashed. "I suppose," she told her family indignantly, "that you're all expecting me to be a good sport and wish Elizabeth a terrific time in Los Angeles." She could hardly get the words out, she was crying so hard. "Well, I don't feel like a good sport." She stood up and pushed her chair into the table, her legs shaky and uncertain. "Elizabeth's your favorite. She always gets everything. She always wins." She turned and, tears streaming, raced out of the kitchen and upstairs to her room.

It didn't help when her mother came up a few minutes later to tell her there would be other trips. And it didn't help when her twin told her that night after dinner that she'd offered once more to trade places with Jessica. "They just won't listen," Elizabeth said and sighed. "I tried telling Mom and Dad that I really wouldn't mind staying, but they say they can't go back on their word."

Jessica, sprawled across her pink and white bedspread, had stopped crying. But she hadn't stopped feeling awful. "Oh, Liz," she asked, "how am I ever going to tell Lila Fowler and The Unicorns? How am I ever going to live this down?"

Even though her sister's problem seemed small beside the real troubles people like Sophia faced, Elizabeth couldn't help feeling sorry. She remembered the hours Jessica had spent singing along with her *Shout* sound-track album.

"Maybe I could get some of the cast to autograph a program for you," Elizabeth suggested. She had to admit that she was beginning to look forward to her big trip. "And maybe I can bring back one of those *Shout* T-shirts."

Jessica looked up hopefully. "That'd be neat, Liz." Then her face resumed the tragic expression it had worn earlier. "It's still not the same, though. Not the same as actually seeing it for myself."

"Well, pretty soon you'll be hard at work on your own show." Elizabeth felt more cheerful as she thought about the school play and all the excitement ahead. "In fact, I phoned Sophia and asked her to come over tonight so we can make plans for the first committee meeting on Wednesday. Maybe you can give us some ideas."

Jessica sat bolt upright. "You're not bringing that girl over *here*! Elizabeth Wakefield, I will never figure you out." She shook her head, and her blue-green eyes snapped back to life. "Besides, I've already invited Lila Fowler over to practice our new cheer."

"So?" asked Elizabeth.

"*So?* So I certainly don't want my best friend to find that creature in our house." Lila was the first cousin of Janet Howell, the Unicorn club president. The very last thing Jessica needed was to have her friend tell Janet that the Rizzos and the Wakefields were getting friendly! "My life is in a shambles, my dreams are shattered, and now you're going to bring that ragtag misfit into our living room!"

"Just a minute here," said Elizabeth. "I thought you were so loaded with math homework that you were going to be up all night. How can you take time out to practice cheerleading?"

Jessica opened her eyes wide until she looked like a big china doll. "Oh, Lizzie," she said in a voice as sweet as honey, "the whole assignment is hateful long division." She stared at her twin with her most helpless look. "You know I was sick the day Ms. Wyler explained it. I was going to ask you if you'd just help me out this one time. I'd never forget it for a trillion years."

"Do you mean you want me to do your homework for you, Jess?" This wasn't the first time Jessica had asked Elizabeth to bail her out of a tough math assignment. But, this time, it was hard to say no. After all, Jessica had just lost the trip of her dreams, and Elizabeth had just won it! "How are you going to learn to solve this kind of problem if I do it for you?"

"But, Lizzie." Jessica pouted and then glanced at her sister out of the corner of her eye. "You're so much better at division than I am. You can do one of those mile-long problems in no time at all. I'd be up all night over something you could get done in five little minutes."

As if on cue, the doorbell rang, and Jessica raced out of the room. "I'll get it. It's Lila." She started down the stairs, but stopped halfway and turned back toward her sister. "Thanks so much, Lizzie. I know I can always count on you when I'm in a jam."

Elizabeth sighed, picked up Jessica's math book, and started through the door to the bathroom that separated the twins' bedrooms. She had homework of her own to do, and it would take some real concentration to get everything done before Sophia came to discuss the play. Still, she felt so guilty about winning the trip to Los Angeles that she was willing to do just about anything to keep Jessica happy. She just had time to sit down at her desk and find a pencil before Jessica rushed into her room.

"Lila and I are going to be practicing in the family room. So, if you must bring that awful girl here, could you make sure you two stay upstairs?"

Guilt or no guilt, Elizabeth became furious at her sister. "Jessica, I don't think you understand. I *like* Sophia. I don't care what you or your snobby club think about her or her family. She's funny and smart and a lot nicer than all the Unicorns put together. In fact," she added, closing the math book and turning to face her twin, "she and I are good friends, and I'm not about to hide it."

This time when the doorbell rang, Jessica stayed frozen to the spot. "Oh, no!" she wailed. "That must be her! And Lila's right downstairs!"

Sure enough, the twins' mother opened the door, and Elizabeth heard a friendly voice say, "Hello. My name is Sophia. I'm a friend of Elizabeth's." When Elizabeth got downstairs, Mrs. Wakefield had shown Sophia into the living room, where Lila was waiting for Jessica.

Elizabeth and Jessica had known Lila Fowler since kindergarten, and Jessica had always liked the spoiled, confident girl a lot better than her sister did. Although Elizabeth admitted that Lila, with her shoulder-length light brown hair and charming smile, was very pretty, the things she said and did were usually far from nice. "Hello, Lila," she greeted Jessica's guest. "Do you know Sophia Rizzo?"

Lila, dressed in a beautiful aqua tennis top and

white slacks, stared at Sophia without speaking. Jessica, finally recovered, raced downstairs to join them. "Hi, everyone," she called gaily, as if nothing were wrong. "Oh, hello, Sophia," she added, turning to Elizabeth's guest as if she'd been expecting her. "I'm glad you came to pick up that box of old clothes we packed. It's good to know they won't go to waste. It's always a pleasure to be able to help those less fortunate than us. See you later."

With that, Jessica grabbed Lila by the arm and dragged her into the den.

"Is that why she thinks I came here?" Sophia turned to Elizabeth in confusion. "To take your old clothes?" Her tiny chin was set firm and hard in her dusky face. "Mama—she—she would never," she began, her voice quivering. "She could never accept charity. She would rather die. She . . ."

"I know," Elizabeth assured her, taking Sophia's hand. "Jessica just got things mixed up." She was too stunned and embarrassed to explain her twin's thoughtlessness. Still confused, Sophia followed her friend upstairs, her dark eyes full of questions Elizabeth didn't want to answer.

Four

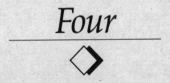

The clock radio and the delicious aroma of her mother's blueberry pancakes woke Elizabeth early on Wednesday morning. She turned lazily in her bed to stare at the ceiling before she remembered that today was the first meeting of the play committee. Suddenly she couldn't get ready for school fast enough. She and Sophia had thought of some wonderful plots for the play, and now she was eager to hear what Mr. Bowman and the others thought of their ideas.

Elizabeth raced into the bathroom. As she brushed her teeth, she listened to the sound of Jessica's clock radio through the door. She knew her twin would be sleeping peacefully despite the loud music. If there was anything Jessica loved more than new clothes, it was sleeping. Elizabeth opened the door and peered at her sister's sleeping form. "Come on, lazybones," she called. "Time to face Ms. Wyler!"

"Ohhhh!" Jessica groaned and rolled over onto her side. "I can't. Thanks to you, I've missed every question on my math homework for two straight days!" Jessica's head disappeared under her sheet. "Ohhh."

"After the way you've been treating Sophia for the past couple of days, you're lucky I'm still walking to school with you." Elizabeth scrubbed her face, then picked up the skirt and blouse she had laid out the night before. "If you think I'm going to teach you long division before you learn to be nice to Sophia, you'd better think again!"

"Lizzie, you know I promised to set things straight, and I will." Jessica rubbed her eyes and sat up in bed. "I'll be as sweet as can be to ragbag today. Boy, from the way you're acting, you'd think *I* was the criminal."

Elizabeth zipped up her skirt and stepped in front of the mirror. "Jess, I'm sure you had plenty of help. After all, the Unicorns could come up with a scheme as nasty as 'accidentally' locking all Sophia's books in the girls' room broom closet!"

Jessica pouted. "Honestly, Liz, you'd think that girl were more important to you than your own sister!"

"Of course not, silly. It's just that I like you both too much to stand the thought of your not liking each other!" She smiled as Jessica walked sleepily into the bathroom.

Her twin joined Elizabeth at the full-length mirror and stuck her tongue out at her own reflection. "Why do you always look so much better than me in the morning, Liz?"

Elizabeth laughed. She studied the two images in the mirror and couldn't see a bit of difference between them, except that one was almost dressed for school and the other still wore a lacy pink nightgown. Both had the same wavy, long blond hair, blue-green eyes, and friendly smile.

"I hate mornings," Jessica complained, trudging back to her room. "I can never find anything to wear." She turned back to glance slyly at her sister. "Oh, Liz, that blouse would go perfectly with my new painter pants!"

Elizabeth paused with the blouse she'd been pulling over her head. "Jessica," she scolded, "if you'd pick out your clothes before you go to bed, we wouldn't have to go through this every day. This blouse also goes perfectly with the skirt I'm wearing!"

Jessica surveyed her closetful of clothes. It bulged with skirts, pants, sweaters, and blouses in every imaginable shade. "I have no decent clothes," she moaned. "Everything I own is disgusting. I'm sick of every single thing!"

"Here." Elizabeth walked over to her twin's closet and selected a pretty top in a cool blue. "This is almost the same color as my blouse. It's just a little darker."

Jessica brightened. "You know, Lizzie, you're right. This will look good." She took the top from Elizabeth and carried it into her twin's room. "In fact, I think it just matches those new earrings we picked out at the mall." She walked to her sister's dresser and reached into the jewel box on top. The earrings she pulled out were covered with blue sparkles and silver beads. She held them up to her ears and smiled into the mirror. "Perfect, aren't they?"

Elizabeth sighed. Both twins had picked out the pretty earrings. But it was Elizabeth's allowance that had paid for them. "OK, OK," she said at last. "But, please, Jess, hurry up. I don't want to be late today!"

By the time the twins arrived at school, everyone had heard the news about the school play. Caroline Pearce, Sweet Valley's biggest gossip, greeted Elizabeth on the steps in front of the big clock. "Hi, playwright," she teased. "What's the play going to be about?" Her straight red hair was pulled back into a tight ponytail that made her green eyes seem even rounder than usual.

"I don't know, Caroline," Elizabeth told her. "We haven't even had our first meeting yet."

"And," Jessica added, "if she *did* know, she certainly wouldn't tell *you*—not unless she wanted it spread all over school."

Caroline wasn't the only student who was curious about the play. As the girls walked down the hall to their homeroom, more and more kids clustered around them, each with a question for Elizabeth.

"Are we doing a musical?"

"Can you write a part for me?"

"You won't let the eighth graders boss everything, will you?"

Jessica was so proud of her sister, she almost forgot to be jealous of all the attention Elizabeth was getting, until Bruce Patman joined the group. "Hey, Elizabeth," the handsome seventh grader said when he spotted the twins. "Congratulations. My dad's going to videotape the whole show, and he says I can have everybody over to watch it."

"Oh, Bruce," Jessica cooed. "*I* think the videotape is a great idea, especially for those of us who're going to have big parts." Compared with the creepy boys in the sixth grade, Bruce seemed very mature and sophisticated to Jessica. She always wondered what it would be like to be a member of the wealthy Patman family and be able to have anything you wanted, no matter how much it cost!

"Well, if you want a good part, you'd better check with your sister here," Bruce told Jessica. "After all, she's the one writing the play, right?" He looked admiringly at Jessica's twin and fell into step beside her as she walked toward her locker. "By the way, I'm a pretty good actor, Elizabeth. How about a major role for Bruce the hunk?"

Elizabeth didn't share Jessica's high opinion of

Bruce. For as long as she'd known him, she'd thought he was silly and spoiled. Just because his father was one of the richest men in town, he seemed to think he was entitled to bully and brag his way through life.

"There are a lot of people on the writing committee besides me, Bruce. We're all working together."

"Yeah," Bruce agreed. "But don't forget to put in something that'll really suit my talents."

Outside their homeroom, the twins stopped and Elizabeth smiled. "I think I've got just the thing," she told him.

"Really?" Bruce and the group of students that had been following him pressed around her eagerly. "What is it?"

"Well, I know how much you like the spotlight, Bruce, so I thought I'd ask Mr. Bowman if you can do the lights for our show!" As the last bell rang, the crowd of kids burst into laughter and scattered for homeroom, leaving Bruce standing by himself in the middle of the hall.

"Hey, Elizabeth, that's the greatest news ever!" Amy Sutton whispered loudly when Elizabeth took her seat. Gangly and thin, with straight blond hair and pale blue eyes, Amy was Elizabeth's best friend. She was also a valuable member of *The Sweet Valley Sixers'* staff.

"Thanks, Amy. We're meeting after school today. I can hardly wait." Suddenly her face clouded as she remembered. "Hey, that means I won't be able to get to our regular *Sixers* meeting. Do you think you and Julie can handle it?"

"Sure," agreed Amy, "Julie and I will take care of everything. Are we still meeting for lunch?"

"You bet." Lunchtime wouldn't be the same, Elizabeth thought, without Amy and Julie Porter, another *Sixers* reporter, giggling and laughing at their usual table in the cafeteria. "I want to get your ideas about the show before the committee gets together."

Amy's face glowed. "Gee, Elizabeth. That would be wonderful."

The rest of the day seemed to drag. It felt like an eternity before Elizabeth, Amy, and Julie were huddled in a corner of the cafeteria, talking over plans for the show. Outgoing and friendly, with pretty red hair and huge green eyes, Julie was a talented pianist and a good writer. She and Elizabeth always got along well.

"I sure hope you write a play we can identify with," Julie confided over their untouched pizzaburgers, a cafeteria special that all the kids at school joked about but almost never ate. "I mean shows like *The Sound of Music* are nice, but what do they have to do with us, with the things we think and do?"

"You're right," Amy agreed. "Why can't we have a show about *us*, about what it's like to be in middle school?"

"That's a great idea!" Elizabeth exclaimed. "I just hope everyone on the committee agrees. I know Sophia will."

"I thought you said those stories she wrote were about fantasy princesses and toads and things." Elizabeth had spent most of the lunch period the day before telling her friends about the stories and plays she'd read at Sophia's house.

"Those were the things she wrote when she was little," Elizabeth explained. "You should read the stories and plays she writes now." Elizabeth remembered the skit about the girl and her baby sister. "I'd say those are close to home. And great, too. I couldn't believe anybody our age could write like that!"

"Speaking of Sophia," said Amy, "where is she?" She craned her thin neck to scan the big, windowed room. "I never see her at lunch."

"I don't know," Elizabeth told them. "I guess she goes home for lunch a lot. Her mother can't get around very well, so maybe Sophia needs to go home and help out."

"Gee, that's rough." Amy looked genuinely sympathetic. "Maybe we could invite her to have lunch with us sometime."

"Sure. Why not?"

"Why not what?" Brooke Dennis, the daughter of a well-known Hollywood screen writer, had just carried her tray to the table. Even though she had gotten off on the wrong foot with all three girls when she first moved to Sweet Valley, she was now a good friend.

"We were just thinking about making Sophia Rizzo a regular member of our lunch group," Julie explained.

"I remember a great place where Elizabeth and I had a picnic lunch right here on the school grounds. Why couldn't we eat there with Sophia?" Brooke asked.

Elizabeth recalled the shady patch of grass behind the gym. "It's perfect!" she declared and smiled approvingly at Brooke. "It makes a great hideaway. In fact, I don't know why we haven't gone back there. We could all bring sandwiches and drinks from home. That way Sophia can bring lunch without feeling left out."

"Terrific!" Amy exclaimed. "I'll bring some of the fruit my aunt just sent from Florida. Mom says it will rot if we don't get rid of it soon."

"Don't forget my dad's potato salad," Julie piped up. "He'd be insulted if he found out we were planning a picnic without his specialty!"

Elizabeth was chosen to deliver their invitation to Sophia that afternoon at the committee meeting. She waited impatiently outside Mr. Bowman's room until she saw her friend. "Hi. I have a secret message for you." Smiling broadly, she handed Sophia a tiny square of paper. It had been folded and refolded until it was not much bigger than a postage stamp.

Elizabeth's smile encouraged Sophia, and after only a moment's hesitation, she unfolded it. Scrawled in fluorescent green on a sheet of bright yellow paper, the note read, "You are hereby invited to a secret outdoor picnic sponsored by the anti-cafeteria lunch group. Thursday at lunch period behind the gym. Bring your own sandwich. RSVP. Amy, Elizabeth, Julie, Brooke."

The look of happy surprise on Sophia's face said everything. For a minute neither girl spoke, then Elizabeth explained how the four friends had cooked up the idea of a getaway picnic. "Everyone's bringing something from home," she told Sophia.

"My mother makes the best fruit punch in the world," said Sophia. "I'll bring a thermos of it and hide it in my locker."

"Terrific. But what about this meeting? Did you bring your play about the two sisters?"

"Yup. And the one about the mother and the girl who wants to stay out late." Sophia sounded confused. "I brought everything you asked me to, but I still don't understand why."

"Because not everyone can write like you, that's why." Elizabeth smiled. "And because I want the committee to know that plays don't have to be about places we've never been or things we've never done to be exciting!"

Sophia smiled. "I just want you to know how much your support means to me," she said, her voice sounding strong and brave. "Even if nobody else on the committee likes my plays, it won't matter. I'm just glad my friend, Elizabeth, does."

"And I'm not the only one," Elizabeth promised her. "Just you wait till the others see your work. Why, you'll be signing autographs all over Sweet Valley!" And, as the two girls laughed and walked into the first play committee meeting, Elizabeth hoped that it was true.

Five

Mr. Bowman and the members of the play committee were seated around a long conference table at the back of the room when Elizabeth and Sophia opened the door. "Welcome," said Mr. Bowman.

Elizabeth didn't know whether to feel relieved or concerned as she glanced at the faces around the table. One of the seventh-grade committee members was Mary Robinson, a slender girl whose pretty features were framed with curly blond hair. Mary was a Unicorn, but not the sort to go along with the club's gossip and teasing. The other seventh grader, though, was a different story. Peter Jeffries was a friend of Bruce Patman's, and any friend of Bruce's, Elizabeth was convinced, would be no friend of Sophia's.

"We started without you," Peter teased them. 'So far, we've decided everything except what to call the show, where to start, and how we can ever be ready in three weeks!"

Mr. Bowman smiled. "Well, I'm sure we'll be making changes even after auditions. If we count rehearsal time, we'll have more than a month to get ready."

"I still think we might be better off using a play that's already been written," complained Lisa Rainish, one of the eighth graders. Elizabeth didn't really know her, but she had a plump, friendly face and was always running for student office. It seemed that Lisa was on every committee in school.

"I think you're just afraid to tackle this," the boy sitting next to Lisa said. His name was Northrop, but all the kids called him Nort the nerd. An eighth grader, Nort was very smart and, Elizabeth guessed, very lonely. He talked in a serious, mature way that made it hard to imagine he ever had any fun. "If every writer felt that way," he scolded Lisa, "no great books would ever have been written."

"Maybe we should take a vote," suggested Mr. Bowman. "I'm afraid I just assumed a student play would be a popular idea, but there's no reason we can't use a professionally written show if you want."

"No!" Elizabeth exclaimed before she could stop herself. Now, though she felt embarrassed, she wasn't about to let the school pass up a chance to give the most special play it had ever presented. "Mr. Bowman, this is really important, and I'm sure all of us want a play that says what *we* want to, not what someone else thinks. It's a wonderful idea, and everyone in school is excited about it."

Lisa still looked concerned. "Oh, it's not that I don't think it's a great idea, Elizabeth. It's just that— Well, what makes you think we have anything important to say? I mean none of us is exactly William Shakespeare."

"That's just why we're the ones who can write our play," insisted Elizabeth. "We're not grown-up professionals, so we're much closer to what it's like to be a kid. I don't think we should try for *Romeo and Juliet*. I think we should write about what's on our own minds. And who can do that better than us?"

Suddenly Peter Jeffries started clapping loudly. At first Elizabeth thought he was teasing, but when she looked at the broad smile on his face, she couldn't help smiling back.

"I think Elizabeth is right," he said. "I think it's about time we spoke up for ourselves instead of always complaining about what we're assigned to read and write in school." He looked in Mr. Bowman's direction, then lowered his head apologetically. "In most of our classes, that is," he added quickly.

Mr. Bowman laughed. "Hey," he told them, "I'm the first to admit that I'm not a kid. No, Elizabeth and Peter are right. If you have something to say, no one else is going to say it for you."

Mary Robinson looked puzzled. "But what do we want to say? All of us are different people. Can we all say something together?"

"Well," considered Lisa, "we do say things together in student council, in a way. I mean we all vote on things. So there must be some things we all agree on."

"That's right," said Peter. "Why, I'll bet if we took a vote on whether or not to stop serving pizzaburgers in the cafeteria, not a single person would say no!"

"And, *I'll* bet that if we all listened to some of the ideas Sophia has come up with," said Elizabeth, "the vote would be unanimous, too."

Everyone at the table turned to Sophia. She was the only committee member who hadn't spoken so far. Now, aware of their eyes on her, she flushed deeply and fumbled with the first few pages in her notebook. For a minute, she looked helplessly at Elizabeth, but her friend's calm smile was enough to give her the courage to speak. "Well," she told them, "I think all of us have families, and that means all of us have family problems."

"You bet!" said Nort. "Has anyone here ever tried living with a father that gets disappointed by an A-minus?"

"Or a mother who insists that all my phone calls be less than three minutes long?" asked Lisa.

"Of course, Sophia, what you're saying is true," said Mary. "But we can all sit around this table griping about our parents and still not come up with a play. I mean, how do you show this stuff on a stage?"

"By showing both sides, I think," Sophia answered. "By letting characters that we all know speak for themselves."

"That sounds OK, but what makes you think we can do it?" asked Peter. He looked interested as he leaned across the table, an earnest expression on his face.

"*I* think you can do it, for one thing." Mr. Bowman looked around the room. "You're excellent writers and creative thinkers. That's why you're here."

"I don't *think* we can do it," added Elizabeth. "I *know* we can." She nudged Sophia, smiling encouragement. "In fact, Sophia's already started for us. Sophia, why don't you read the scene about the girl who wants to stay out late."

Blushing with embarrassment, Sophia sat motionless at the table. Elizabeth turned Sophia's black notebook to the page she wanted.

Sophia began to read slowly, her voice uncertain, but as she read on, she became calm and sure. Even though Elizabeth recognized Sophia and her mother in the characters, it didn't matter. As she and the others listened to the dialogue, it could have been about any girl and her mother. The scene was a short one, just a brief argument between the two over staying out too late for a movie, but it was filled with all the detail and complications of real life.

Sophia finished reading and shut the notebook, still blushing furiously.

There was nothing but silence at first. Mr. Bow-man didn't say a word, but sat with his head bent as if he were still listening to Sophia. The others stared at one another as if they couldn't believe what they had heard. It was Nort who finally broke the still-ness. "Wow!" he said, adjusting his dark-framed glasses. "That might not be Shakespeare, but it cer-tainly is *us*!"

Suddenly everyone was talking at once. They had lots of ideas now, experiences from their own lives, things they wanted to add. Sophia's play had opened them like a key, and all at once their feelings were pouring out. Elizabeth studied the animated faces around her. Then she glanced at Sophia's small, dark face, shy and smiling in their midst. Somehow, she wasn't sure why, Elizabeth felt she was watching a miracle.

Even on the way home, walking with Sophia, the feeling that something special had happened re-mained. "You know," she told her friend, "that's what I always thought writing was all about. The way you helped everyone see themselves more clearly, the way you made them interested in every-day things." She stared in open admiration at Sophia. "It's just what I hope I can do someday."

"It's just what you did today." Sophia laughed, as happy as Elizabeth had ever seen her. "If you hadn't said what you did about speaking for our-selves, they never would have listened to me in the first place."

"We make a great team." Elizabeth smiled, re-membering the way the committee, especially Peter Jeffries, had heaped praise on Sophia. Maybe she'd been wrong to assume that a friend of Bruce would be just like him. "With my mouth and your talent," Elizabeth told Sophia, "there's no telling how far we can go!"

Sophia paused at the turnoff to her own street. "Don't you dare make fun of yourself that way, Elizabeth Wakefield!" she scolded gently. "It's a talent to like people and to make them like themselves. And if you never write another word, you'll still be the most talented person I know!"

Elizabeth watched her friend hurry down the street toward her tiny house. Then, she, too, turned toward home, feeling relaxed and happy. Today had been exciting, but it was just the beginning. The committee had decided to continue Sophia's short play, to explore the theme of parents and children by telling the story of one family. Even though it meant no splashy musical numbers, they wanted to present their ideas as realistically as possible. And they were determined to make sure that most of the play was completed for the auditions in three weeks.

Elizabeth was so intent on the committee's plans and on getting ready for their next meeting, that she hardly noticed how quiet the kitchen was. Usually she could count on arriving home to the sight of Steven stuffing his face or a rousing argument between her sister and brother. This time, though, the stillness should have alerted her. But it wasn't until she opened the refrigerator door that Elizabeth knew something was wrong.

There was still plenty of snack food on every shelf. Steven not hungry after school? It didn't seem possible! Shrugging, she grabbed an apple from the fruit bowl and started upstairs. She met her brother on the bottom step.

Steven, uncharacteristically quiet, was hunched on the last step, his head in his hands. "Hey," Elizabeth joked, "this must be serious. There's a whole piece of Mom's chocolate cake left! What's up?"

"What's down is more like it," Steven told her, lifting his head to reveal a black eye. "And the answer was me. Flat on my face."

"Steven!" Elizabeth cried, reaching over to hug her brother. He looked so miserable and hurt, she didn't know what to say. "How did it happen?"

"Ask your good friend's brother," Jessica answered for Steven, appearing suddenly on the upstairs landing with one eyebrow raised and a disapproving frown. "Anthony Rizzo strikes again!"

Elizabeth stared at her brother's bruised eye. It had turned red and bloodshot, while the skin around it was dark and swollen. Had Sophia's brother really done this?

"I was standing with a group of kids when, pow, knockout city," Steven told her. "I mean just about everyone in the group was saying things about Tony. I sure wasn't the only one."

"Maybe now you'll choose your friends a little more carefully," Jessica warned Elizabeth. "Just wait until Mom and Dad hear about this!"

Elizabeth knew her parents were having dinner with one of Mrs. Wakefield's clients. What *would* they say about this? she wondered. "I'm sure they know better than to judge people by association," she told Jessica. "Anthony Rizzo is one person, and his sister is another. The person, in fact," she couldn't help adding, "who has just been chosen to be head writer for our school play."

"What?" Jessica exclaimed, outraged. "You mean we're going to let a criminal's sister write our play?"

"If you mean Sophia, that's right. And it's not going to be some silly musical either. It's going to be a serious drama."

Jessica was furious. "This is just too much. First, I lost the chance to go to the greatest show ever written, and now I lose the chance to star in my own school play!"

"Who says, Jess?" Elizabeth asked. "You can still try out for the show. There'll be plenty of really good parts."

"Not good enough for me, Liz," declared Jessica. "If you think for one minute I'm going to have anything to do with a play written by the sister of the juvenile delinquent that punched my brother, you're nuts!"

"But Sophia isn't responsible for what her brother does," Elizabeth insisted, angry and surprised at Jessica's reaction. She got up and went into the kitchen, opened the refrigerator, and emptied the ice tray. A minute later she was back with a handful of cubes wrapped in a dish towel.

"Steven," she asked, "are you sure you didn't do anything special to make Tony Rizzo mad? Why on earth would he pick you out of the crowd to hit?" She held the towel out to him and watched as he put it against his eye. He flinched as he felt the cold.

"I told you, Liz. Nothing worse than the rest did. I was just agreeing with what Larry Harris said.

A projector is missing from the AV Room." He shifted uncomfortably as his eye felt colder. "After they made the announcement in assembly this morning, a whole group of kids began blaming Tony. Larry called him Hot Fingers. I said that we should check his books for burn marks. Then a couple of guys started to try to get his science book.

"Things were sort of getting out of hand, so I tried to stop them. I remembered how you said we shouldn't judge Tony without a fair trial, so that's what I said. The next thing I knew, he hit me!"

"Oh, Steven, I'm sorry."

"You're sorry!" Steven shook his head. "You don't have to walk around looking like a monster!" He paused and looked at his sister. "Even if I didn't prove anything to Tony Rizzo, that punch of his sure taught *me* a lesson."

Elizabeth felt awful. She didn't see how the black eye could have taught her brother anything at all. "What?" she asked gently.

"Never to listen to you, that's what!"

Six

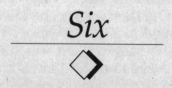

At breakfast the next morning, Elizabeth felt nervous. Steven and the twins had gone to bed before their parents came home from dinner, so no one knew how the Wakefields would react when they saw Steven's black eye. Hoping her mother and father wouldn't be so mad at Anthony Rizzo that they'd be angry at Sophia, Elizabeth waited for her brother to come downstairs to the kitchen table. Like Jessica, he was never cheerful in the morning. Sometimes he skipped breakfast altogether.

It looked as if today would be one of those times. Even Jessica appeared and picked at her cereal. Still, Steven remained upstairs. Between spoonfuls, her twin gave Elizabeth smug grins and kept whispering, "Just wait! Wait till they find out!"

But Elizabeth couldn't wait. She had promised to meet Julie and Amy before school to fill them in on the previous day's committee meeting. "I'll bet," she whispered to her sister as she scooped her books up from the counter, "I won't miss a thing. I'm sure you'll fill me in on all the details anyway."

Elizabeth knew Jessica wouldn't miss Steven's grand entrance for anything. She kissed her parents and started out of the kitchen, then looked back to see her twin rooted to her chair, waiting with the same I-told-you-so look she had worn the night before.

At school, though, the excitement of the show soon made her forget about Steven. Everyone wanted to find out more about the play, and Elizabeth hardly had a minute to herself until lunchtime. And, although Jessica called over to her as she and Amy walked by the cafeteria, Elizabeth could only wave back and hurry outside with her best friend. On top of everything else, today was the day of their picnic with Sophia, and she didn't want to miss the fun of sharing a secret lunch.

Sure enough, Julie, Brooke, and Sophia were waiting for them at the back door of the gym. The five girls couldn't help giggling. All of them were loaded down with picnic supplies. Each carried a paper bag, while Sophia hugged a giant thermos and a package of paper cups. "Who said getting out of eating school food was easy?" Brooke joked, leading the way toward a toolshed that stood near a huge elm tree behind the school.

Sophia, looking as happy as if she'd been invited to a royal ball, followed the others until at last they stood under the arching branches of the elm.

"You see how perfect it is?" Elizabeth asked her. "The toolshed hides us from sight, and we can pretend that school doesn't even exist!"

Sophia looked around the cool, green nook under the tree. "It's too good to be true!" she said, her eyes wide with pleasure. She set the thermos on the ground and unwrapped the cups.

"I'd like to propose a toast," Julie announced as soon as the cups were filled and each girl had taken one.

"Great," said Amy, her long blond hair curling a little in the gentle wind. "What shall we drink to? The play? I just know it's going to be terrific."

"No," answered Julie. "Let's drink to the first official picnic of the anticafeteria lunch group."

"But not the last," added Brooke, raising her cup. "I think we should sneak away like this every week, all of us."

Sophia's eyes were filled with pleasure as she sipped her punch and watched the other girls. She stood very close to Elizabeth as if she thought her new friend might suddenly vanish into thin air.

"Terrific idea, Brooke," Elizabeth declared. "Let's make Thursday our regular picnic day. OK?"

"Me, too?" Sophia asked hopefully.

"Of course, Sophia," Amy told her. "You're a member of our group."

Soon all five were sitting comfortably under the tree with a large flowered sheet spread between them. "I just hate to eat without a tablecloth," admitted Julie, who had spirited the sheet from her mother's linen closet. Next, the feast was set out—sandwiches, pickles, cold pizza, potato salad, and, for dessert, fruit and cookies.

"This feels like a birthday party," exclaimed Brooke. "It's hard to believe we could be having so much fun so close to school!"

"Well, we still have a long time until a real birthday party," observed Julie. "I think Amy's is next, and that's still months away." She stopped and looked at Sophia questioningly. "Unless, of course, your birthday is sooner, Sophia. I know everybody's birth date except yours."

"Oh, mine's coming up next month," Sophia told her. But, instead of looking happy at the prospect of a birthday, Sophia seemed suddenly depressed. It was as if a shadow fell across her face. "Birthdays only come once a year," she said, sounding more cheerful. "But this picnic can happen any time we want. Why, we can almost make school disappear just by meeting here." Her dark eyes glowed with new sparkle and mischief. "In fact, when I lie back in the grass like this I don't even remember how to diagram a sentence."

"Hey," said Brooke, leaning back beside Sophia and staring up at the sky, "you're right! Why I've even forgotten who Ms. Wyler is!"

The others tried, too, sprawling on their backs and watching the branches of the elm trace patterns against the clouds. "What does the Hairnet look like?" said Elizabeth, giggling as she thought about Mrs. Arnette. "I've forgotten her face."

"And her social studies class, too," said Julie. She leaped up and brushed crumbs from her skirt. "I'm afraid that's the bell."

Everyone stopped and listened. Sure enough, in the distance, they heard the bell ringing. "Gosh," complained Amy, "why is lunch period always so short?" She stood up and collected pieces of paper and stray cups from their tablecloth. I guess we'd better go back inside."

"I hate to leave," Sophia said sadly. "We had so much fun here."

"Don't worry," Elizabeth reminded her. "You're an official member of the anticafeteria lunch group now. That means you've got a date here once a week. Right?"

The second bell rang, and the little group packed up quickly and raced back toward the school. Just as they opened the gym door, Sophia touched Elizabeth's arm and whispered, "Thanks for the nicest school lunch I've ever had." Then she laughed, brushing at her moist eyes. "It really did feel like a birthday party—I think."

"What do you mean you 'think,' Sophia?" Elizabeth asked. "Haven't you ever had a birthday party?"

Sophia's curly dark hair framed her blushing face. "Not really," she admitted. "You see, Mama's never been able to give a party for me. Besides, even if I gave it myself, no one would come." She studied the ground, unable to meet Elizabeth's eyes. "That note from the Unicorns wasn't the first, Elizabeth. Ever since I've been old enough to go to school, I've been getting notes like that from kids." With a tremendous effort, she finally raised her eyes and looked at her new friend. "That's why today was so special."

Elizabeth was used to elaborate parties with balloons and music and lots of presents. It was hard for her to imagine that Sophia had never once known what it was like to have a real birthday celebration. "If you think I'm going to let your birthday pass without an honest-to-goodness party," Elizabeth declared, "you don't know me very well, Sophia!"

"But I didn't mean—"

"Don't you dare say a word. Just meet me in front of the office after school." She grabbed her friend's wrist and made Sophia look at her. "Promise?"

Sophia's eyes dropped. "All right," she whispered so low that Elizabeth could barely hear her.

Elizabeth was full of plans. By the end of the day, she could hardly wait to find out exactly when Sophia's birthday was. But before she could keep her appointment with her friend, Jessica rushed over to her. "I've got to tell you what Mom and Dad told Steven," Jessica insisted.

"It can wait," Elizabeth told her sister firmly. "I have to talk with Sophia after school. It's important,

Jess. You and I can talk as soon as I get home, OK?"

Jessica's blue-green eyes narrowed. "You mean you're choosing that disgusting creature over your own flesh and blood?" Her voice rose, and she pointed a finger right in Elizabeth's face. "Don't say I didn't tell you, Elizabeth. Believe me, you'll break Mom's and Dad's hearts if you keep hanging out with that tacky family!"

Elizabeth watched her sister stamp angrily down the hall toward the front steps of the school. Just as Jessica was storming down the stairs, Sophia started up them. Elizabeth watched in dismay as her sister and her friend passed each other without a word. Sophia tried a smile when she saw Jessica, but Jessica brushed angrily by her. At the bottom of the stairs she turned back toward Elizabeth. "As long as you're going to be talking to Hot Fingers' sister," she announced loudly, "you might as well tell her to try putting on a play with no one in it."

Elizabeth and Sophia stared as Jessica disappeared from view. "What did she mean?" asked Sophia. From her confused expression, it was clear she had no idea what had happened between her brother and Steven the day before.

"We'll talk about *that* later," Elizabeth told her as they left the building. "Right now we have some important planning to do. Let's walk home, and I'll tell you about your party on the way."

"My party?"

"Sure. We're going to throw you the biggest, best birthday party ever—at my house!"

Sophia stopped in the middle of the sidewalk to stare at her friend. "Oh, Elizabeth! Do you really mean it? Gee, everybody would come to a party at *your* house." She blushed. "Even if it was for me."

"So when's the date?" Elizabeth was already excited at the prospect of giving Sophia her first birthday party. "I just hope it's not before the play!"

"No, thank goodness. It's the day after our Friday performance!"

"Terrific! We'll have two reasons to celebrate on Saturday! We'll invite the whole cast. We'll invite everybody!"

Sophia looked happy, but a little worry line creased her brow. "It sounds like a dream." She sighed. "But could we keep it small, just the people you think might really like to come?"

"Of course," Elizabeth declared. "But, remember, you'll be a famous playwright by then, and everyone will be *dying* for invitations."

Both girls laughed, but Elizabeth was serious about her belief in Sophia. "I mean it, Sophia," she said. "If the story you've started turns out to be half as good as I think, a lot of things will change for you at school. Of course," she added, "there's a lot of work to do."

All the way to Sophia's house they talked about the play. They discussed characters they thought should be added to Sophia's stage family. Sophia's story was missing a father and Elizabeth had insisted that their play needed one. "When Dad's away on a trip," she explained, "we all miss him like crazy, especially Steven."

"I know what you mean," Sophia agreed, sadness returning to her voice. "Before my father left, Tony was happy and good. Mama never had any trouble with him, and I always had someone special I could talk things over with." She stopped at the door to her house, putting one finger over her mouth. "We'd better not talk about this anymore, Elizabeth. Not around Mama. It makes her sad to remember how Tony used to be."

Elizabeth had wondered earlier if she should tell Sophia about what her brother had done to Steven. Now, ushered into her friend's kitchen for an after-school snack, she decided not to mention the fight yet. The two girls had been in Sophia's room for over an hour when they heard Mrs. Rizzo open the front door. "Tony," they heard her say, "you're home early."

Maybe it was the memory of Steven's bruised eye or all the rumors she'd heard. Whatever the reason, Elizabeth was not anxious to meet Anthony Rizzo. "Uh, I have to go home now. It's getting late," she told Sophia. "We'll finish tomorrow, after the committee meeting." Hurriedly, she gathered her books and headed for the front door just as a tall boy walked into the living room.

Elizabeth had seen Tony Rizzo only once before, but she recognized him immediately. He had brown eyes like his sister's, but his face was sullen and sharp. Tony stepped back a bit when he saw Elizabeth, and his angular, dark-skinned face took on a guarded look.

"Tony," Sophia told him, "this is my friend Elizabeth. Elizabeth, my brother, Tony." She stood back, smiling shyly, as if she hoped they would like each other on sight. But, as Tony Rizzo grudgingly held out his hand, Elizabeth felt a rush of confusion and anger. The boy standing before her was her new friend's brother. Yet the hand she was shaking was probably the same one he'd hit her brother with. Was Jessica right? Would it break her parents' hearts to know she was here?

Turning toward the door, Elizabeth stammered in embarrassment. "I—I really have to go, Sophia. I have a lot of homework. See you tomorrow." Her cheeks burning, she bolted out the door and down the Rizzos' walk. It wasn't until she got to her own street that she stopped running and started thinking.

Could she be making the same mistake about Tony that everyone at school had made about his sister? Maybe there was just an ordinary person somewhere under that rough manner. Maybe a little kindness would bring back the loving brother who used to help Sophia before their father left. Maybe, she told herself as she reached her front door, she would discuss this with Sophia tomorrow. They could talk everything over and get it all straight.

And that was exactly what Mr. Wakefield said as soon as Elizabeth had dropped her books on the kitchen counter. "There's something we have to talk about," he said, pulling out a chair for her at the table. Mrs. Wakefield sat beside him. Both her parents looked serious.

"Is this really a conference?" she asked nervously. "Shouldn't we get Steven and Jessica?"

"No," Mr. Wakefield said quietly. "We've already talked with them. In fact, it was your sister who told us you have a particular interest in the Rizzo family."

Elizabeth had been dreading this moment. Now, she was so anxious to convince her mother and father that Sophia was a wonderful, talented girl that everything came out at once. She told them about the work her friend had done on the *Sixers*, about the wonderful plays she'd written, about Mrs. Rizzo's bad leg.

As Elizabeth tried to tell them how she felt about her friend, her father folded his hands and finally interrupted her in a quiet, forceful voice. It was the voice his children called his "courtroom voice." It meant that everyone else listened. "Your mother and I have made a decision, honey. We're going to ask you to stop seeing Sophia outside of school. Jessica tells us you've spent quite a lot of time at her house."

"But, Mom, Dad, Sophia shouldn't be punished for what her brother did!"

"It's not a question of punishing," Mrs. Wakefield declared. "It's a question of protecting *you*."

"That's right, Elizabeth," her father continued. "You know I don't deal with juvenile criminal cases, but Tom Bradford in our office does. He handled the Rizzo case when the boy was brought up on burglary charges two years ago. From what he says, that young man has some serious problems."

"But, Daddy . . ." Elizabeth couldn't believe her ears. Her parents had always told her not to listen to rumors, and to make her own decisions about people. How could they ask her not to see a girl who'd been in their house only once? "You don't even know Sophia!"

Mr. Wakefield put his hand on Elizabeth's

shoulder. "Tony Rizzo is trouble, and his home isn't the sort of place where we want to see our daughter. We're not telling you that you can't speak to Sophia or see her in school. We're merely asking that you don't socialize with her outside of school."

Elizabeth tried to interrupt again, to tell them about Mrs. Rizzo's warm, neat house, about how much she cared about both of her children, but Mr. Wakefield raised his hand. "I'm afraid this decision isn't open to debate, Elizabeth. I've looked at the court records, and I've seen your brother's face. That is quite enough to convince me we're better off keeping our distance from the Rizzos—*all* of them."

Elizabeth sank into her chair, feeling tears sting her eyes. She knew from the sound of her father's voice that no arguments, tears, or pleas would change things. It meant that her birthday party for Sophia would have to be canceled. And tomorrow she would have to give her friend an excuse for not visiting her anymore.

Seven

Jessica poked her head into her sister's room, anxious to learn how Elizabeth's discussion with their parents had gone. She found Elizabeth stretched full-length on her blue corduroy bedspread.

"You look like someone just died," said Jessica.

Elizabeth didn't feel like talking to anyone, especially Jessica. She was probably the one who had convinced her parents that Sophia was a bad influence. "Look, Jessica, you got things just the way you wanted them, so don't pretend to be sorry now."

"For your information, big sister," Jessica assured her twin, "I did my best to help." Without being invited, she sat beside Elizabeth on the bed, moving her twin's feet to make room. "I told Mom and Dad that you just don't know any better than to trust everyone, even hardened criminals."

"Wow, that's great. Thanks for the favor. Is there anything else you want to do for me?" Elizabeth rolled over to look at her twin. "Do you really think that, Jess? Do you really think I'm wrong about Sophia?"

Jessica hugged Elizabeth. "Don't you see, silly? I'm not worried about Sophia; I just care about you. If someone's going to save Sophia, let it be anybody else. Why should you be the one?"

"But if everyone feels that way, then no one will ever give her a chance, even people as terrific as Mom and Dad."

"Well, I'm glad they've put the Rizzo place off-limits. I don't want my only twin spending all her free time with the creepiest family in Sweet Valley." Jessica glanced at her sister. "Now, do you forgive me or not?" Her smile was mischievous and irresistible. "If you do, I've got some good news about your trip to L.A."

"OK, Jess." Elizabeth sighed and hugged her sister. "Let's call a truce." She hated it when they were mad at each other, and she knew it was impossible to hold a grudge against Jessica. "What's up? In all the excitement over our school play, I'd almost forgotten about *Shout*."

"How could you?" Jessica declared, shocked. "How could you think some embarrassing sob story written by the—that *person*—could be more important than the greatest show ever created, Liz?" She shook her blond head. "Sometimes I think you and I live on different planets!" Then, smiling, she slipped a piece of paper into Elizabeth's hand.

"What's this?" Elizabeth unrolled a lined sheet covered with Jessica's big, careless handwriting.

"It's a fan letter. To Terrence Wesley, the actor who plays Holt. Since I won't be able to go, and since Dad says you'll be going backstage, I want you to give it to him."

When Elizabeth began to read the letter, Jessica became embarrassed. "Oh, Liz, you're not supposed to read that. It's personal. It's silly, I guess, but I just wanted him to know how absolutely perfect he is."

"You mean we're actually going to talk to the cast?" Elizabeth couldn't believe her ears. "Mr. Martin must be a real VIP." Elizabeth carefully folded the letter and put it on her table. "Of course I'll give him your note, and I'll tell him it comes from his biggest fan!" She genuinely wished her twin could give her letter to the star herself. After all, no one cared more about the show than Jessica.

"And if you don't tell me exactly what color his eyes are, Elizabeth Wakefield, I'll never forgive you! I want you to pay attention to every detail. I want to know absolutely everything, how he walks, how he talks, how he shakes hands."

Elizabeth laughed. "Maybe I should just take a video camera into his dressing room!"

"I'm serious, Liz. I expect a full report." Jessica stood up and then walked toward her room. "I'm just glad that awful play of Sophia's will be over the day before, so you can concentrate on the really important show!"

"The day before. You mean the trip is the Saturday after our play?"

"Of course, silly. Don't you have it marked on your calendar?" Suddenly she frowned, remembering how all her plans had gone wrong. "First I circled the day of the play, but now I'm not going to try out after all. Then I circled our trip, hoping Mom and Dad would let me go, but now that's off! I just hope the Mini-Olympics don't fall through, too!"

Elizabeth felt terrible. She was scheduled to go to Los Angeles on Sophia's birthday! How could she have forgotten? Things were worse than ever. Slumped on her bed, she only half-listened to Jessica's chatter about her brand-new scheme.

"Since I wouldn't be caught dead in that gross play, I've decided to concentrate on getting chosen chairman of the Mini-Olympics." The Mini-Olympics was an annual day-long festival of races and games that the sixth grade helped organize.

"That's great, Jess," Elizabeth told her twin. "But if I don't get this homework done, you'll have to change all your plans to attend my funeral!"

"I can take a hint!" Jessica left, shutting the bathroom door behind her and Elizabeth tried to get back to work. But after she'd read the same paragraph in her social studies book three times, she closed the cover. Why had things worked out so badly? Why couldn't her parents understand how much more Jessica wanted to go to Los Angeles than she did? Now that she knew the trip was scheduled for Sophia's birthday, she would give almost anything to stay home. After all, Mom and Dad were going on the boat trip that day, so if Elizabeth were home, she could at least spend some time with Sophia. She could show her that someone really did care.

The next morning at breakfast, Elizabeth decided to make one more try. "Mom," she asked, "couldn't Jessica *please* take my place on the trip? You know she's the one who deserves to go."

"Elizabeth, I thought we'd already settled this. This trip isn't a prize to the best twin, or even the person who most wants to go." Her mother glanced briefly at their father, as if looking for support.

"Your mother's right," Mr. Wakefield responded. "The Martins have room for only one guest. It's a lucky chance that the ticket became available, and we all agreed that luck would decide who went." He looked at Jessica, who, her breakfast untouched, had been holding her breath in the hope that her sister's plea would succeed. "When this family makes a decision together, we all have to abide by it. Jessica, I'm sure you and Steven can find something fun to do while your mother and I are away."

Jessica's face collapsed into a frown that made it plain spending the day with her brother was not her idea of a good time. Steven spoke up. "Sorry to break your heart, sister dear," he told her, "but I've got a date with a basketball. The coaches have invited the team to a post-season game and party that day. Even if we don't win this weekend, Coach Horner says he wants to thank us for a great effort. And, if we do win, he's going to throw the biggest victory celebration ever! So it looks as though you'll be home alone!"

All during school the next day, Elizabeth wondered how she was going to avoid going to Sophia's house that afternoon. The two had planned to discuss the play after the second committee meeting. The worst part of all was having to hide the truth. She couldn't tell Sophia what her parents had done.

They walked back to Sophia's house after school. As Sophia led the way to the door, Elizabeth said, "Gee, I'd like to come in, Sophia," hoping she didn't look as uncomfortable as she felt, "but I—I've got this funny feeling in my stomach." She searched her friend's face to see if she suspected anything. "And—and my throat feels kind of itchy."

"Gosh, that's too bad, Elizabeth," said Sophia, concerned. "You seemed fine at our meeting. Why don't you go home now. Maybe, if you feel better later on, you could sketch out some dialogue for the second scene."

"Only if you promise to give it your special finishing touch. I could never make the characters as real as you do. I'll call you soon, OK?" At least no one could stop her from talking to Sophia on the phone, she thought miserably.

"Great." Sophia, turning up her driveway, smiled and waved. "And don't forget," she added, "we still have to plan our guest list. I don't know which I'm looking forward to more, our play or our party!"

The heavy, guilty feeling grew so strong that by the time she reached home, Elizabeth thought she might really *be* sick. Even Steven noticed her mood. "Hey, Mistress of Gloom," he greeted her from beside the refrigerator, "why so low?"

Although she wanted to tell someone how horrible it made her feel to listen to Sophia talk about the birthday party, there was no one to confide in. Steven, whose black eye had turned a sickly yellow, was the last person who would understand. "I don't know," she told her brother. "I guess I wish Jessica could go to L.A. in my place."

Elizabeth doubted there was any solution to her problems, but she was open to suggestions. "OK, big brother, do you have any answers?"

"Simple." Steven smiled, wrinkling the yellow skin under his right eye. "The old switcheroo."

"What?"

"You know. Change places. You be Jessica, and Jessica will be you. After all, you do look exactly alike. And it wouldn't be so tough to pull the wool over the Martins' eyes for two days. After all, they've never even met you two. Besides it's all in a good cause." Steven stood up, his plate clean, and grabbed his basketball jersey from a hook on the kitchen door. "If we have to keep listening to Jessica whine and carry on about that darn show, the whole family's going to go nuts!"

Even after Steven had gone upstairs and she heard the loud beat of his stereo through the ceiling, Elizabeth continued to sit quietly in the kitchen. While Jessica always enjoyed switches and intrigue, Elizabeth disliked doing things behind her parents' backs. Still, her brother's suggestion did seem like the way to make everyone happy, even Sophia. With the family away for the weekend, maybe she could have a small party for her friend. She'd invite only a few good friends, and it could stay a secret: a special secret for a special girl.

There was one problem, of course, and Elizabeth decided to face it right away. If Jessica wasn't willing to go along with the switch, it was no use planning Sophia's party. As she hurried upstairs and knocked on her twin's bedroom door, she realized she mustn't mention the birthday party. If Jessica thought she was helping Sophia by going to Los Angeles, she might even be willing to give up seeing her favorite show!

"Come on in," Jessica called. "You're just the grammar expert I need to see!" Jessica was lying across the foot of her bed, surrounded by two apples, a bag of potato chips, and an English book. "How do you diagram a preposition anyway?"

"Oh, Jess! You're not going to ask me to do your English assignment, are you?"

With a huge grin and round, innocent eyes, Jessica looked up at her twin. "Now, Liz," she said in a voice like honey, "would I do a thing like that?" Then, her grin spreading, she added, "But come on in and let's have a sister-to-sister talk."

Elizabeth, sitting on her twin's bed and kicking

off her shoes, wondered what else, besides an English assignment, Jessica's trip to Los Angeles was going to cost her.

Eight

◆

"What? You want to switch places!" Jessica was so surprised she forgot all about getting Elizabeth to help with her homework. Although she was always full of sneaky schemes, her truthful sister was the last person Jessica expected to suggest such a plan. "Weren't you the one who gave me that goody-goody lecture after our triplet trick fizzled?"

"But this time is different, Jess," Elizabeth insisted. "It's not as if we'd be hurting anyone else." *In fact*, she added to herself, *we'd be helping someone, someone who wants a birthday party just as badly as you want to see* Shout. "Mom and Dad are leaving for their boat party first thing in the morning, and the Martins won't pick me—uh, you—up until noon. Everything will work perfectly."

"What about our blabbermouth brother?" asked Jessica, making room for her sister beside her on the bed. "Steven isn't exactly famous for keeping secrets."

"This whole thing was *his* idea. Believe me, Jess, he wants to see you happy just as much as I do."

Jessica tossed aside her English book, interested

now. "Sometimes that jerk makes me think he's an actual human being," she admitted, a twinkle in her eyes. Suddenly, though, her eyes narrowed. "Wait a minute, Liz. Steven wasn't even invited, so he doesn't lose anything if I go to Los Angeles. But, what about *you*? I know you're the best sister ever, but still, why would you give up such a neat trip to the city? After all, you won it fair and square."

"Oh, it's not that I don't *want* to go," Elizabeth assured her twin. "It's just that you want to go *more*." She glanced at Jessica, who still looked suspicious. "Besides," she added, reaching for a potato chip, "I'll still be unwinding from the excitement of Friday night. Don't forget, that's the opening night of our big play."

"Your big play, maybe. Not mine. And not anybody else's, if I have anything to say about it." Jessica folded her arms and glowered. "*I'm* not going to auditions next week, and I'll bet not a single Unicorn will try out either."

"Jessica Wakefield, don't you dare spoil this play! It's going to be the best thing the school has ever done. You've got just the talent we need to make the show a success. Why not at least read it before you make up your mind?" Elizabeth scrambled off her sister's bed and started out the room. "I've got some scenes in my desk. I *know* if you read them, you'll see what I mean."

But before her twin had reached the bathroom that connected their rooms, Jessica was calling her back. "Don't bother, Liz. I won't read a word of that disgusting girl's play, and I *won't* make a fool of myself by being in it." Jessica looked so angry and determined that Elizabeth gave up and returned to the bed.

"All right, Jess. Suit yourself, but please don't make up everybody else's mind. Maybe some of your friends would feel different if they came to auditions and listened to our play."

"Are you serious, Liz? If you think anybody would want to be involved with that shabby Sophia or her stupid play, you're dead wrong. Why there's not even going to be singing or dancing! It's going to be too embarrassing to even watch! In fact, the Unicorns have already decided not to go."

"No! Jessica, you don't mean it! You can't!"

"I can and I do. If that play ends up with no cast and no audience, you won't see me crying."

Elizabeth knew Jessica could be hasty and hurtful sometimes, but she never dreamed her twin would go to such lengths to snub someone who'd never harmed her. "Jessica, I've met Tony Rizzo. And, even though I can hardly believe he's related to someone as sweet as Sophia, that could never make me stop liking her. You've got to give her a chance," she pleaded.

"Like the one that her brother gave Steven? No way!" Jessica cried. She got up from her bed and walked toward Elizabeth's closet. She stood by the door, scanning its contents. "Now, let's talk about something more pleasant, like what I—uh, I mean— you are going to wear to *Shout*."

Elizabeth watched her sister pick through her best dresses and skirts. If she was going to get out of Los Angeles, she knew that now was not the time to try to talk Jessica out of her campaign against Sophia.

After Jessica had selected two dresses, a scarf, and a gold necklace, she joined her sister for a cram course in sentence diagraming. The twins spent the next forty-five minutes working. Although she fidgeted and squirmed, Jessica was a quick learner. The next morning she surprised both Elizabeth and Mr. Bowman by being the first in class to finish one of his "pop" quizzes.

"I'm impressed!" Elizabeth whispered as the bell rang. "I didn't know you were such a whiz at English."

"It's easy when you've got a good teacher." Jessica winked at her sister and gathered up her books. "See you later, Liz. I've got a rush Unicorn meeting."

"I hope you all don't get stiff necks from holding your noses up in the air," Elizabeth teased.

"I heard that, Elizabeth Wakefield." Lila Fowler joined the two as they left the room. She was wearing a yellow jumper with a coordinated print blouse. Her hair looked as perfect as everything else about her. "For your information, the Unicorns don't turn up their noses at anyone unless they're second rate." The smile she beamed at Elizabeth was as cold as it was pretty. "It's just that all the first-rate people are already Unicorns."

"Except for one, of course." Jessica hugged her twin affectionately. Even though she knew Elizabeth could never enjoy the kind of gossip and intrigues the Unicorns loved, her sister was still her favorite person. She dumped her books in Elizabeth's already loaded arms, then waved gaily. "Since you're going that way, Liz, would you throw my books in your locker? I'll pick them up after lunch." Without another word she grabbed Lila's arm and rushed off down the hall.

As the two girls raced away from Elizabeth, a third student raced toward her. Smiling and waving, Sophia was so anxious to get Elizabeth's attention that she didn't watch where she was running. In horror, Elizabeth watched as Lila and Jessica collided head-on with Sophia. Lila's books and the arm-load of papers Sophia had been carrying went sailing as all three girls tumbled to the floor.

"I might have known," Lila said when she saw who had run into them. Her face was calm, but there was no mistaking the sarcastic tone in her voice. "Here, let me help you up, Sophia. We wouldn't want to spoil that designer gown, would we?"

Too stunned to be hurt by the cruel remark about her simple dress, Sophia let Lila pull her to a standing position. Then she stooped down and began retrieving the papers one by one. Before she could reach the last page, Jessica grabbed it and waved it in front of her fellow Unicorn.

"Oh, what have we here, Lila?" Jessica asked. "Look at this, everyone," Jessica shouted. "We've been bowled over by the school play, knocked down by the biggest talent in Sweet Valley, maybe even the world."

While Sophia reached frantically for the page, Jessica continued to wave it around. Soon a crowd of curious students gathered around them. Suddenly, Lila grabbed the sheet of paper from Jessica, held it in front of her, and announced grandly, "And now, I think we should sample a bit of this great play we've all heard so much about. I'll just audition right now."

One boy laughed loudly, and someone else applauded as Lila started speaking in a ridiculously dramatic voice. "'Mom,'" she read, "'I couldn't tell you how I felt before.'" She rolled her eyes and put one hand on her chest. "Have you ever heard such meaningful dialogue?" she asked the crowd around her. "I think my heart is breaking!"

She looked once more at the page she held and began reading again. "'Sometimes being a kid is the hardest job of all.'" Now she fell to the floor as if she'd been shot. "Oh, the power of feeling here." She groaned. "I can't stand to go on!" Her eyes still rolling, she lay on the floor as if she'd fainted.

Lila's hand fell to the floor, and the paper she'd been reading fluttered out of it. Sophia, tears of humiliation streaming down her face, scrambled to pick it up. Then without a word she ran down the hall, clutching the crumpled sheets of the play. Elizabeth tried to stop her, but the girl streaked past as if she were running in a race.

Lila wasn't finished. She loved being the center of attention, and more than a dozen people were clustered around her, giggling and talking. Slowly she sat up, then stood to more applause. "Thank you. Thank you. I know none of us can wait to hear more of that tragic story. I mean, who needs a fun musical with great dancing and singing when we can have one of Sophia Rizzo's tragedies?"

Elizabeth watched helplessly as Sophia's hard work was spoiled with a few cruel words. She had hoped Jessica might try to stop Lila's thoughtless antics, but her sister almost never crossed Lila, and she would never take sides with Sophia!

It wasn't hard to find Sophia. Seated alone at the table in Mr. Bowman's classroom, Sophia was crying, her small round face buried in her hands. When Elizabeth touched her shoulder, Sophia looked up with an expression that would have broken anyone's heart. "It's over," she sobbed. "The play's over before it began."

"It is not," Elizabeth told her firmly. "You'll see. We don't need the same old people who keep trying out year after year. We'll use people who don't usually get the chance, kids more like the ones in the play."

"But everyone will hate it. They were all laughing. Didn't you hear them?" Sophia was choking, and her words came in spurts from crying so hard. "Everyone always laughs at me. They laugh at my clothes. They laugh at my house. They laugh at Tony, too, even though he tries to scare them all." She made an effort to stop sobbing and looked steadily at Elizabeth. "I think that's why Tony changed, just to stop them from laughing. He thinks he can beat the laughter out of them. He even hit a boy in school the other day. He doesn't know they're laughing harder than ever. He doesn't know they'll never stop." This time she couldn't hold back, and the tears came uncontrollably.

Elizabeth got a terrible feeling as she listened to her friend. "This boy your brother hit," she asked, "what was his name?"

"I don't know. What does it matter? He was just someone else laughing, someone else making fun.

Tony's still on trial in this town. He'll never be able to pay for what he did two years ago. They'll never let him."

Elizabeth sat quietly with her arm around her friend's shoulders. It was clear Sophia was crying for her family as much as for herself. Finally, she stopped and sat up. She tried to explain, but the words came slowly.

"He used to be so happy, so much fun. He used to be my best friend. He helped around the house, and whenever we'd get discouraged, he would tell us how everything would work out fine. He—he made us proud to be Rizzos."

At first Elizabeth didn't understand. "You mean your father, Sophia?"

"No, Elizabeth. My father was never a real father to me. He never made me feel proud. I—I mean Tony. Tony the way he used to be before Papa left us. Sometimes, on a good day, I think maybe he'll change again, maybe things will get better. But then he comes home with that fierce face and anger in his eyes. And then I get scared, Elizabeth, so scared I'll never get my brother back."

Elizabeth was still. She knew Sophia was too proud to have told her all this before. She knew, too, that she couldn't hurt her friend again when, tears still glistening in her brown eyes, Sophia asked her to come home with her after school. "I need a friend to talk to, to tell me it's going to be all right. If you're there, working with me on the play, I'll believe it, Elizabeth. By myself, I'll give up."

"Sure," Elizabeth told her, knowing she couldn't bring herself to play sick again. Even if it meant disobeying her parents, she had to visit the Rizzos' that afternoon. "The two of us have a lot of work to do. We've got a play *and* a party to get ready!"

Nine

Elizabeth found it harder and harder to obey her parents where Sophia was concerned. As much as she loved her mother and father and hated lying to them, she came to count on her after-school visits at the Rizzos'. During the week before auditions, the two girls worked together almost every afternoon. And each visit made them closer friends than ever.

"If it wasn't for your help after these committee meetings," Sophia told Elizabeth the day before try-outs, "I don't know how I would have managed to finish this last act." She brushed her brown hair back from her forehead and slipped her arm through her friend's. "And now, I think we deserve a celebration. How about two orange frostees at Casey's Place? Mama told me I could use the Rizzo raffle money to treat you."

"Rizzo raffle?" Elizabeth looked confused. "Does your family run a contest?"

"Sort of." Sophia's eyes were full of merriment. "You see, all week long Mama, Tony, and I put all of our change into the cookie jar in the kitchen. Every

Saturday, we each try to guess how much is in the jar. Whoever comes closest picks our Sunday trip." She smiled. "If there's not much in the jar, we may just buy marshmallows and toast them on the beach. Once, when we had a lot, we took a bus ride to the aquarium!"

Elizabeth thought the Rizzos' contest was a wonderful idea. "Maybe we could start a Wakefield Wheel of Fortune at home," she said. "The only trouble is, Steven would always pick the same prize, a round-trip for one to Guido's Pizza Palace!"

"Your brother sounds funny," Sophia said. Suddenly, her smiled faded, and she turned serious. "I wish Tony would laugh the way he used to. Lately, he doesn't seem to have any sense of humor at all. Maybe Steven could teach him something."

"Well, uh, maybe," Elizabeth answered, then quickly changed the subject. "But let's not use the Rizzo raffle money for frostees. Let's make our own right here at your house." Elizabeth didn't want Sophia to spend her money at Casey's. And, just as important, she didn't want Jessica or any of the Unicorns to spot them at the popular after-school hangout. Elizabeth wasn't sure what would happen if word got back to her parents.

"OK." Sophia smiled and led the way into the Rizzos' tiny kitchen. "I know a terrific recipe for lemon slush."

Breathing a sigh of relief, Elizabeth set to work. Soon Mrs. Rizzo joined them, and all three bustled around the room, crushing ice, getting glasses, and preparing a tray to take into the living room.

When they had settled around the old trunk

Mrs. Rizzo used as a coffee table, the play was on everyone's mind. Even though her English wasn't very good, Sophia's mother was full of questions about Sophia's drama. "I have heard only bits and pieces so far," she explained to them. "What is this fine play all about?"

Sophia hugged her mother. "This fine play is about us, Mama!"

"Us?" Mrs. Rizzo looked surprised and a little worried. "You mean you and me—and Tony?"

"Not exactly, Mama. It's about a family. Anybody's family. Everybody's family."

"We call it *Straight Talk*, Mrs. Rizzo," Elizabeth volunteered. "Everyone on the committee got so excited about Sophia's ideas, we decided to make the play about one family, a family everyone could understand. There's a mother, a father, two sisters, and a son."

"Even some next-door neighbors and friends," added Sophia. "Once we got started it was hard to stop!" Her face was brightened by the enthusiastic smile Elizabeth had come to love. "Now we've got so many parts in the play, Mr. Bowman thinks we should invite the high school drama club to come to tryouts. He's afraid that even eighth graders might be too young for the parents' roles."

"I hope he doesn't ask the older students to come," added Elizabeth. "I want this to be *our* play, and I think we have plenty of kids who could play those parts."

"*If* they haven't been talked out of trying out." Sophia's look was enough to remind Elizabeth that her own twin was trying to sabotage the play.

"What do you mean?" Mrs. Rizzo asked. "Why wouldn't they want to try out for the play?"

Elizabeth stirred her lemon slush and tried to explain things as gently as she could. "I think a lot of kids still want a slick Broadway play about some fantastic dreamworld." She winked at Sophia. "Not everyone wants to take a good, close look at the world they really live in."

"Well," Mrs. Rizzo concluded, rising slowly to take the pitcher back to the kitchen, "if we are ever going to make dreams come true, the only way is to start with what we've got." She smiled broadly at the two girls. "And we've got quite a lot, right? You just wait until tomorrow. When you read them your play, those kids will be fighting for a chance to be part of it, Sophia."

Elizabeth saw the pride in Mrs. Rizzo's eyes. She knew that play or no play Sophia already had all the applause she needed at home! Still, she told herself, it would be wonderful if the play committee could present their work to a big, enthusiastic crowd of actors.

But it didn't happen. Just as Elizabeth and Sophia feared, Jessica and the Unicorns had spread the word. There were only a handful of students waiting in the auditorium after school the next day. Mr. Bowman, who had helped Peter Jeffries run off posters to announce the tryouts, was perplexed. "Didn't you put up the announcements we wrote, Peter?" he asked.

"I sure did, Mr. Bowman. Mary and I put them everywhere we could think of." Peter, who had probably heard about Lila's "audition" from Bruce Patman, looked unhappy and embarrassed. "I—I'm really sorry, Sophia," he said, sounding as if he were to blame.

"That's OK," said Sophia. Elizabeth could tell from the way her voice trembled that she was hurt. "I guess there were a lot of other meetings today."

Mary Robinson, who knew what the Unicorns had been up to, couldn't bear to see the work all of them had done for weeks wasted. "I think it's terrible!" She turned away from the stage and looked behind the front row of chairs, where the committee sat. There were no more than ten boys and girls in the nearly empty gym. "What are we going to do? We have more parts than players!"

"No we don't." Nort seemed to surprise even himself by taking things firmly in hand. "Just because we haven't got enough people here doesn't mean there aren't enough in the school." He no longer sounded shy and retiring. "I think we should go ahead and cast a few roles today and then give a reading next week during English class."

Mr. Bowman agreed that scheduling readings during each class he taught would be an excellent way to recruit more actors. "One or two key scenes should be enough to convince your classmates this is a fine play," he told them. "We can cast some of the parts today, as Northrup suggests, and use committee members to read the rest."

"Great!" Peter was smiling and already full of optimism again. "Once they hear this play read *right*, everybody will want a part. In fact," he added, smiling at Sophia, "there's a part I'd like to try out for."

"Me, too," admitted Lisa Rainish. "And, if you don't mind my saying so, Sophia, I think you'd be terrific as Randi, the eldest daughter."

"I'll read Randi," Sophia offered shyly, "if Elizabeth reads her sister."

Suddenly the room was alive with enthusiasm and activity. Mr. Bowman called the names of the students who wanted to audition in alphabetical order. One by one, they walked up onstage to read from the play's final act, the scene Lila had made such fun of the week before. But how different this reading was! Without Lila's dramatics, the characters sprang to life, and the situation seemed so close to home.

The scene brought all the members of the play's family together onstage at once. At first, the dialogue featured some realistic and funny arguments between the parents and their children. Suddenly, toward the end of the scene, there was a surprising tender moment when everyone realized how little they had been saying to one another. Then they all promised to talk straight, to say what was on their minds. It wasn't a happily-ever-after fairy-tale ending, but it was the sort of finale this honest, truthful play seemed to call for. Apparently everyone listening agreed, because when Caroline Pearce, playing the mother, read the final line, everyone in the room burst into spontaneous applause.

Elizabeth realized happily that Mrs. Rizzo wasn't going to be Sophia's only fan. The students who had come to audition were as proud of the play as the committee that had written it. Everyone was so anxious to talk about the story and characters that it wasn't until two hours later that Mr. Bowman was able to dismiss the actors and call the casting meeting to order.

"I think we got a good start on building our stage family today," Mr. Bowman told the committee. He agreed with the others that Caroline, Sweet Valley Middle School's resident gossip, made an excellent mother. Caroline's prissy attitude seemed perfect. "There's no need to bring in high school students with local talent like that," their teacher assured them.

"There'll be a lot more talent to choose from after we read some scenes in English class," Northrup added. "I only hope we'll be able to recruit someone good for the father's character. We didn't really see anyone who could handle it today."

"That's right," agreed Lisa. "But," she added, looking with open admiration at Peter, "we did find a terrific brother."

The hearty cheers of the other committee members made the decision unanimous. Peter had surprised them all. His reading had been one of the best they'd heard. "Thanks," he told them, blushing.

"I think we've made real progress so far," announced Mr. Bowman. "I also think we uncovered more than one new talent this afternoon." He glanced at Sophia, then addressed the entire group. "I'm not sure it's fair that one person have so many gifts, but I *am* sure it wouldn't be fair to our show if anyone else but Sophia played Randi."

Now the applause was amazing. The students clapped until their hands ached. Gentle, shy Sophia had proven herself one of the finest actresses they had seen!

Smiling and proud, Sophia accepted their applause and then made a few suggestions about changing the last scene. Something in the lines had bothered her, and she wanted the scene to be perfect for the readings the next week. "If it's OK with you," she told the others, "I think Elizabeth and I can get it patched up. When she reads to me, I can feel what's right and what's not."

"When she reads, it sounds great to me," Peter told them. "In fact, I think Elizabeth should play your sister. You two are perfect together."

Again, the committee was in agreement. Even Lisa, who had hoped for the sister's part herself, admitted that there was a wonderful interplay between the two girls. "Yes," she said, "they sure do sound like real friends."

"Well," said Elizabeth, "I'm afraid that's not because I'm a good actress. It's just because we really *are* friends."

The next week was a busy one for the committee and for Mr. Bowman. On Monday, every English class featured a brief reading from *Straight Talk*, by Sophia Rizzo. Even though the committee had helped revise and rewrite Sophia's material, they all agreed she deserved credit as the writer. Just as Peter had predicted, by Tuesday there were more than enough students clamoring for parts. The biggest surprise of all, everyone admitted, came when Bruce Patman tried out for the role of the father.

"Wow!" exclaimed Northrup, leaning toward the other committee members, "Isn't he great?"

Elizabeth, suspecting that someone had urged Bruce's involvement, turned to Peter. "With a little help from our friends," she said, smiling, "this play is really shaping up."

Peter smiled back. "I just thought it would be a shame to waste Bruce's natural talents," Peter told them. "After all, he loves telling everyone what to do. I thought he'd make a great parent!"

When Elizabeth got home that afternoon she found her twin fuming. "Why is everyone making such a big fuss over this dumb play?" Jessica exclaimed, looking up from her nails. Elizabeth noticed that she had painted them pink and had glued a tiny, sparkling sticker at the top of each. "Just what is so great about a whole lot of boring words strung together without a single song or dance?"

"I think the fuss is about something pretty different and pretty special, Jess," Elizabeth explained, sitting on her sister's bed. "I sure wish you had tried out, but I'm glad at least one of us will get to watch it."

"Sorry, big sister," Jessica began to wave her hands in order to dry her nails. "I have no intention of attending that play. I'm going to be much too busy getting ready for my trip."

"But everyone's coming," Elizabeth told her, knowing how her sister hated being left out. "Even Lila told me she decided to come and watch Bruce and Peter."

"Count me out," Jessica said with a pout. "I'd rather die. There's positively no way I'm going. There is absolutely and completely nothing anyone can do or say to drag me to Sophia's play!"

"What if someone were to tell you she wasn't going to switch places with you for the trip?" Elizabeth suggested shrewdly.

"Elizabeth Wakefield! That's not fair!"

"Well, it's not fair for you to be so mean to

Sophia when everyone else has decided to give her a chance." Elizabeth smiled, looking almost as crafty as Jessica did when she was hatching a new scheme. "And I suppose that since you won't be switching places with me, you won't want to take my new shoes to Los Angeles with you."

"You mean those little white pumps?" Jessica's eyes lit up.

"Yep." Elizabeth grinned and waited.

"Well," Jessica considered slowly, "maybe I *could* drop by the night of the play. I mean, just to take a tiny peek."

Ten

As the night of the play approached, Elizabeth saw less and less of her family. Except for the day that Steven's basketball team won their league championship and they all celebrated at Casey's together, Elizabeth was seldom home. Rehearsals started after supper and lasted until bedtime. That meant that she usually fell into bed, too exhausted for even a nighttime chat with her twin. After a while Jessica gave up opening her sister's door and trying to share the latest gossip.

But Jessica never dreamed just how busy her sister really was. As the night of the play got closer, so did Sophia's birthday. And, for Sophia at least, the party was as important as her stage debut. "Oh, Elizabeth," she said as the two drew a funny invitation for each guest, "now that I know the kids on the committee and in the cast, I have real friends to invite to my first real birthday party." She looked at Elizabeth, her smile coming easily now. "You said things would change, and they have. How can I ever thank you?"

"By having a terrific time at our party, of course," Elizabeth told her, wishing more than anything that she could tell her parents about it. It made her feel guilty to be in a play about honesty at school, but not to be able to level with her folks at home. Still, as the big day approached, she didn't dare risk Sophia's dream by telling them. What if they forbade her to have the party? How could she ever face Sophia again?

So the invitations were mailed, the last days of rehearsal passed, and, before she knew it, Elizabeth was standing backstage on the night of the performance! Fortunately, Jessica had kept her promise. As Elizabeth peeked out from behind the curtains, she saw her family seated in the second row of the auditorium.

"Everyone's out there!" she whispered to the rest of the cast. "It's a full house!"

"Don't tell me about it!" wailed Sophia, looking pale.

Elizabeth touched her friend's shoulder gently as they watched more people file into the crowded auditorium. "Hey, don't you dare worry. Everything's going to be fine."

"But I've never acted in public before." She began to pace. "What if I forget my lines? What if I get sick right onstage?"

Elizabeth had to admit that her stomach, too, was doing flip-flops. As she studied the sea of faces in the audience, she almost wished the Unicorns hadn't gone back on their threat to boycott the play. She knew the play was good, but what if they weren't as good as they had been in rehearsal? "My dad says all great performers get stage fright," she told Sophia. "Just like horses before a big race." Elizabeth loved horses and had read lots of books about them. "They whinny and jump against their stalls, but then, once the race starts, there's no stopping them."

Elizabeth was right. Even though she seemed nervous and unsure of herself backstage, something happened to Sophia when she played her part in front of the audience. Just as she had at auditions and rehearsals, she made everyone believe in Randi. The world she had written about came to life on the stage. And it was clear that the audience could hardly take its eyes off Sophia as her story unfolded.

And she wasn't the only one. Everyone performed beautifully, and as the cast lined up backstage for the curtain call, they all felt the tingling excitement of a job well done. Holding their breath, Elizabeth and the others who played smaller parts held hands and walked onstage. Immediately, they were greeted with roars of approval and hearty applause. Next it was time for Caroline and Bruce, the mother and father, to take their bows. As they joined the others standing in front of them, even louder applause was heard. Elizabeth saw Bruce's smile as he bent from the waist, just low enough to keep an eye on the audience and relish the reaction.

Finally, it was Peter and Sophia's turn. As they strode onto the stage and stood in front of the cast, the auditorium seemed to go wild. Elizabeth looked at her family in the second row. The Wakefields were applauding with the rest. Their broad smiles told Elizabeth that her parents' feelings about the Rizzos hadn't kept them from enjoying the show. Even Jessica, Elizabeth noticed, was clapping heartily. Sitting beside Steven, her twin laughed when their brother put his fingers to his mouth and let out a piercing whistle.

Then the most special moment in the evening happened. As Sophia stepped back and joined the cast, a man at the back of the room stood up and yelled, "Author! Author!" Soon others in the auditorium were on their feet, too. "Author!" The cry sounded louder and louder. "Author! Author!"

Mr. Bowman whispered from offstage, smiling. "You'll have to take another bow, Sophia. Go on. You've earned it."

Sophia, overwhelmed, stood still where she was. Peter and Bruce, however, acted quickly. Standing on each side of her, they took her arms and gently walked her forward once more to center stage. Now the entire audience was on its feet, and the applause was like an ocean's roar washing across the glorious night.

Later, just before she drifted to sleep, Elizabeth reviewed the day's events. So much seemed to have changed. Sophia had won the respect and admiration of the same boys and girls who had teased her all year long. On the ride home from the play, Steven, whose black eye had healed, decided he shouldn't have judged Sophia so harshly just because of her brother. "I guess," he had said, "that she packs a punch, too. But in a pretty good way!"

"You won't get an argument on that from us," Mr. Wakefield had said. "You were right about one thing, Elizabeth. Sophia has a lot of talent."

"I was close to tears during that last scene," their mother had remarked. "How about you, Jessica? Didn't you enjoy it?"

"I still say she dresses like a toad," Jessica had grumbled from the backseat beside Elizabeth. Then, her blond head tossing impatiently, she added, "But, I guess anyone who can write and act like that can dress any way she wants!"

Elizabeth had leaned over and hugged her sister. It had made her happiest of all that Jessica, the one person who meant more to her than anyone, could admit she'd been wrong.

Snug in her bed, Elizabeth savored the wonderful feelings. Things seemed to have gone so well that she wondered if she should tell her parents about the birthday party the next day. They had been moved by Sophia's play. Didn't that mean they'd be willing to reconsider their request that Elizabeth stop seeing Sophia? Maybe she should ask their permission to give the party. But, she decided as she dozed off, why take a chance? She would have to explain about the switch and might ruin Jessica's chance for her dream trip. No, it was best to go ahead with her plans, even though she felt like a sneak. She would make up for it the following week by explaining everything.

Next morning Elizabeth woke to the sound of Jessica's hair dryer. She looked at her clock radio. It was ten o'clock! Her mother and father had left for the beach two hours earlier, and Steven was supposed to meet his team at nine. The Martins were due to pick up "Elizabeth" any minute!

Sleepy, but still feeling proud and happy from the night before, Elizabeth stumbled into Jessica's rooms to see if she could help. "It's a good thing the Martins don't know us too well," she joked. "Or those suitcases would be a dead giveaway."

Elizabeth was a careful traveler, and her family marveled that she could fit what she needed for the longest trips into a single overnight bag. The secret, she often told Jessica, was organization and advance planning. But Jessica didn't follow her sister's advice. Today, Jessica's three suitcases bulged and overflowed with enough clothes to last several people for a week!

"I think it's going to take both of us to close this one," Elizabeth said, smiling. She walked to a large open case that was filled to the top and over. She examined the clothes her sister had packed. "Jess, do you really need to take *four* pairs of shoes?"

"Of course," insisted her twin, turning off the dryer and joining Elizabeth next to the yawning suitcase. "What if I change my mood when I get there? Or what if the Martins' daughter is not dressing up? Or if it rains? Liz, I've simply got to be ready for anything."

"Well, you better be ready quickly, because that

sounds like a car in the driveway right now." Sure enough, when they raced to the window to look down at the driveway, both girls saw a black limousine pulling up to the house.

"Oh, goodness, I'm not ready! You've got to stall them, Liz!" Jessica began racing wildly around her bedroom, snatching up a hairbrush and barrettes. "Oh, whoever thought they'd be early?"

Elizabeth continued to watch from the window as an elegantly dressed woman and a girl about the twins' age stepped from the car. The girl had short dark hair and was dressed in a stunning glazed cotton sundress and jacket.

It's a good thing Jessica's going instead of me, Elizabeth thought as she studied the girl's stiff, snobbish expression. *She has a lot more patience with spoiled brats than I do!*

The doorbell rang, and Jessica sat down on the last suitcase, hoping her weight would force it closed.

As the doorbell rang again, Elizabeth hopped on the suitcase beside her sister. Together they succeeded in getting the lid closed and locked. Then Elizabeth raced down to the door while Jessica gave one last look around her room to make sure she hadn't forgotten anything. She spotted her cast album and remembered she wanted Terrence Wesley to autograph it. She dashed to her night table and grabbed the album. Finally, glancing at the giant *Shout* poster over her bed, she blew a kiss in its direction. "Goodbye for now, Terrence," she whispered. "See you soon!"

When Jessica reached the foot of the stairs, Mrs.

Martin, her daughter, and their driver had joined Elizabeth in the living room. "And this is my sister, Elizabeth," Jessica heard her twin announce. She greeted the two visitors, feeling her excitement rise as she noticed the beautiful clothes they were wearing. *This is going to be an absolutely perfect weekend*, Jessica told herself, *if I can just remember that my name is Elizabeth!*

Mrs. Martin explained that her husband was waiting in the car and that they had to hurry. The driver helped the girls get Jessica's luggage and then, after Elizabeth gave her sister a quick kiss goodbye, the limousine headed out the drive. Elizabeth stood, waving at the tiny silhouette in the backseat until the car pulled out of sight. She hoped the trip would be special.

Elizabeth stood alone in front of the house for only a minute before she remembered there was no time to lose. She had already alerted Amy and Julie, and they were waiting for the phone call that would mean they could rush over to start decorating for Sophia's party. "The coast is clear," she told Amy when she answered her phone. "Operation birthday is ready to roll!"

After she had called Julie, Elizabeth set to work herself. She had only a few hours, she reminded herself, to bake a cake and shop for enough food to feed the cast. Steven would be gone all day, and her parents weren't due back until after dinner. Her brother had promised to tell them that Elizabeth had gotten safely off on her trip, and that Jessica had been so lonely and depressed she'd gone to Lila Fowler's house to spend the night. Elizabeth would spend the night with Amy after the party. The party had to be over and all evidence cleaned up by six o'clock!

Once Amy and Julie arrived and all three girls were busy hanging festive streamers of turquoise and pink crepe paper across the dining room, Elizabeth felt glad she had offered to host Sophia's party. Quickly the room was transformed into a magic place, fit for a special celebration. Along one side, the girls arranged party hats and silly noisemakers. The hats were all pointed clown hats except for Sophia's. *She deserves to be treated like a real princess for once,* she thought to herself as she placed a silver foil tiara in the center of the row of hats.

Along the other side of the room was a long table lined with plates and trays. Soon these dishes were heaped with doughnuts, pretzels, and taco shells and fixings. Tall pitchers waited to be filled with soda, juice, and, of course, lemon slush. Best of all was the cake. Elizabeth and Julie worked hard on the finishing touches. Finally they brought it in for Amy to inspect.

"Ooooh!" she exclaimed. "It's just beautiful." On the cake's top, in chocolate and strawberry frosting, Julie had sketched a stage, complete with billowing pink curtains. Between the curtains, Elizabeth had written, in cherry frosting, "Happy Birthday, Sophia."

As she studied their handiwork, Elizabeth knew all the plotting and planning had been worth it. She could just picture Sophia's face when she saw the beautiful room.

Amy seemed to understand how she felt. "This is going to be a new start for a new friend," she announced, glancing with satisfaction around the gaily decorated room. "I'm sure your mom and dad would understand."

"I hope so," Elizabeth told her. But, as the doorbell rang and the first guests began to arrive, Elizabeth felt a twinge of guilt. After all, this was the first party either twin had ever given without their parents' permission. Even Jessica had never done anything so sneaky!

Eleven
◇

While Elizabeth and her crew were hard at work, her parents were in their car, heading back to Sweet Valley. A sudden storm had changed their plans and forced the boat party back to dry land. As the car wound down the shore highway, Mrs. Wakefield remembered how disappointed Jessica was when Elizabeth had been chosen to go with the Martins.

"I know we did the right thing by sending Elizabeth to L.A., Ned," she told her husband. "Still, I felt awful about leaving Jessica alone today with nothing to do. I'm glad we'll have a chance to make it up to her."

"It was lucky the Sloans' children invited that group of teenagers over," said Mr. Wakefield. "I think bringing Jessica back to the party with us is just what the doctor ordered."

"You're right, honey. There's nothing Jessica enjoys more than a party. And now we can all spend the day together." As they approached the downtown area and turned toward Sweet Valley's residential section, both Mr. and Mrs. Wakefield were thinking that things usually had a way of working out for the best.

That wasn't at all what Elizabeth was thinking as she watched guest after guest come into the house. She had deliberately invited just a few people so that Sophia's party could be a secret from her parents. But now came not only the cast members who had been invited, but dozens of boys and girls who suddenly wanted to be Sophia's friends.

"Where's the birthday girl?" asked Lila Fowler, brushing past Amy and joining the crowd in the dining room. She was wearing a purple flared skirt and matching soft-knit sweater. She carried a box wrapped in a bright purple paper and ribbon that Elizabeth was sure she had picked to match her outfit!

"The Rizzos don't have a car," explained Elizabeth. She looked pointedly at Lila, who had probably been dropped off by her father's chauffeur. "She should be here in a few minutes."

"Say," said Peter. "That'll give us time to hide." He smiled apologetically at his hostess. "I know it's kind of corny, Liz, but since Sophia's never really had a birthday, I thought—well—"

"I think it's a great idea, Peter! OK, everyone. Find a place to make yourselves invisible, and when we open the door, let's hear the biggest Happy Birthday cheer ever!"

Instantly, the Wakefield house was alive with activity, as over forty kids scrambled for hiding places, behind the sofa and chairs in the living room; in back of the buffet in the dining room; even wedged between the coatrack and table in the hall!

Watching everyone run for cover, Elizabeth wondered what had happened to the quiet party she'd planned. "Where did they all come from?" she asked. "I told the cast to keep our party quiet, but it looks like word leaked out."

"*Gushed out*, is more like it," commented Amy. "I think everyone sort of feels they discovered Sophia last night. I hope she doesn't mind so many people hogging her limelight."

"If I know Sophia," Elizabeth assured her, "she'll be only too glad to share her success with so many friends. In fact, today may mean even more to her than last night."

When the doorbell rang a few minutes later, Amy hushed the crowd. "OK," she told them. "Everyone in the world is here except Sophia. That must be our birthday girl, so stay out of sight."

Everyone ducked, and cries of "Quiet!" and "Shhh!" sounded. Exchanging grins, Elizabeth, Amy, and Julie raced to answer the door. Then, as the crowd of guests roared "Happy Birthday!" everyone stood up in time to see a very surprised Mr. and Mrs. Wakefield walk into the hall!

Elizabeth stared in disbelief at her parents. All her plans had been so careful. She'd thought of everything—except the possibility of her parents coming home early. "What—what are *you* doing here?" she asked before she could stop herself.

"We might ask you the same thing, young lady." Mr. Wakefield stared at the crowd of embarrassed, silent children. "What on earth is going on?"

"Why aren't you in L.A.?" Mrs. Wakefield asked. "Where's Jessica? We came to take her back to the party with us."

Elizabeth felt numb. Tears filled her eyes as she tried to explain. "Jessica wanted to go to L.A. so badly," she told them. "She was the one who really deserved that trip. So we . . . switched places. But it was all my idea, honest." She could hardly look at her parents. Her words tumbled out as she tried to make them see how important the party was for Sophia.

"I never meant to lie to you. Oh, Mom, Dad, I—I just wanted to give her a real birthday party. Her first one ever." Through her tears she saw all the kids in the room watching her. Her face felt hot as a blush crept into her cheeks. "I promised Sophia a party long before you told me I couldn't see her, and I just couldn't break my promise. I had to show her someone cares. She's never done anything to hurt anyone. I—I was going to tell you, but things got so complicated so fast. They just kept getting worse and worse."

"Please, Mr. and Mrs. Wakefield. We're so sorry," said Amy. "We'll clean up this mess right away. Before you know it, everything will be just the way it was."

Before Elizabeth's parents could say a word, everyone went to work, taking down decorations and returning food to the kitchen. But only a few bowls had been put in the refrigerator and a single streamer torn from the ceiling when the doorbell rang again. The guests held their breath as Mrs. Wakefield opened the door and Sophia Rizzo walked in.

When she saw the crowd of guests and the colorful decorations, Sophia's face lit up into a dazzling smile. "Oh!" she gasped, as if she had walked into a fairy tale. She looked from one face to another, and then from the sideboard heaped with party hats to the table covered with food. "Wow!" But as her eyes met Elizabeth's, she realized something was dreadfully wrong. "What is it?" she asked, going immediately to her friend's side.

This was without a doubt the most awful day in Elizabeth's life. And the worst was still ahead. It was bad enough to confess in front of all her friends what a horrible mess she'd made of everything. It was bad enough to think that her parents might never trust her again. But now she knew she would have to call off the party and ruin everything for Sophia. Her voice hardly above a whisper, she said to her friend, "I—I have something to tell you."

"We all have something to tell you, Sophia," Mr. Wakefield interrupted. Then, smiling at his wife, he asked her, "Don't we, honey?"

"We sure do," Mrs. Wakefield agreed. She moved beside the guest of honor, putting her arm around her. "Happy birthday, Sophia!" she said.

Elizabeth could hardly believe her ears. "But I thought you said—"

"What we said was wrong," her father explained. "If there's one thing we all learned from Sophia's play it's that everyone makes mistakes, grown-ups as well as kids."

"Not that you didn't make a pretty big one

yourself, Elizabeth Wakefield," added her mother. "Next time I hope you'll trust your parents enough to let them in on your plans." She smiled just enough to let Elizabeth know she was forgiven but not entirely off the hook.

Even though she knew there was probably a well-deserved punishment in store, Elizabeth felt wonderful: Her parents weren't going to punish Sophia for Elizabeth's mistake. In fact, thanks to her father, it looked as if the Rizzos were about to get a second chance.

"Why don't we make this a family affair?" Mr. Wakefield asked Sophia. "I could drive over and pick up your mother." He paused and looked at Elizabeth, who smiled back gratefully. "And your brother, too, if he'd care to join us."

Surrounded by more friends than she had ever dreamed of, Sophia could only smile and nod happily. It was Elizabeth who answered for her. "That would be wonderful," she told her father. And, as she watched him wave to her friends and head for the door, she felt warm all over just to know that she had such a kind, understanding man for her dad.

Elizabeth knew why her father was driving to the Rizzos. It was his way of showing her that he intended to check things out, to make up his own mind without listening to gossip and rumors. And once he had met Mrs. Rizzo and gotten to know Sophia, she knew things would be set straight.

Sure enough, a half hour later, just as Sophia was cutting her birthday cake, Mr. Wakefield walked in accompanied by Mrs. Rizzo. Sophia, who had her back to the door and didn't see them come in, was intent on avoiding the pink iced curtains Julie had worked so hard on. "I can't bear to cut them," she confessed. "I don't want the curtains to close on this day—ever!"

"I don't blame you a bit," Mrs. Rizzo said, stepping up to hug her. "And if I wore a crown like that, I would never want to take it off."

Sophia was indeed wearing the pretty little tiara Elizabeth had bought for her. Turning, she smiled at her mother. "Mama! Look!" She whirled around with delight, modeling the crown. "Have you ever seen such a big head in your life? This crown is going to pop right off if I get any happier!"

"Your head is not so big, Sophia," her mother told her. "You deserve it all, everything." Small and shy among the guests, Mrs. Rizzo blushed and hugged her daughter again. "Tony, he—he didn't come, but he feels just the same. Really he does, Sophia."

A shadow crossed Sophia's face for a minute, but then passed like a cloud in the wind. "I know he does, Mama," she whispered. "I know he does."

As happy at Sophia's triumph as if it had been her own, Elizabeth grabbed a cup and raised it high in the air. "And now," she announced, giggling in spite of herself, "I'd like to propose a toast."

Laughing and jostling one another to get closer, her schoolmates gathered around her. "What are we drinking to, Elizabeth?" Caroline Pierce asked, her cup poised.

Elizabeth looked at her parents and at the ring of smiling faces around her. Finally, she caught Sophia's eye and winked. She remembered the secret picnic, the committee meetings, and her afternoons at the Rizzo home. "To friends," she said, grinning broadly around the room. "To times we'll never forget."

Next it was time for Sophia to open her presents. And what presents they were! One of the guests had placed the play program in a metal frame engraved with the date and Sophia's name. Bruce Patman presented her with a neatly wrapped videotape of the entire production. "That's just a copy," he confessed. "My dad insisted on keeping the original for himself. You can come over and watch it whenever you want to."

"Well, my present has nothing to do with the play," said Lila Fowler, "but you have to open it before I explode!" Lila did indeed look as if she couldn't wait until Sophia opened the purple package. She handed it with great ceremony to the guest of honor.

Elizabeth eyed the package suspiciously. But Sophia was too happy to hold a grudge. Shyly, she whispered her thanks and took the present on her lap. When she had opened the box, she lifted a beautiful purple sweater from the tissue. It was nearly identical to the one Lila herself was wearing.

"I thought that as long as you're going to be famous," Lila told her, "you might as well dress like someone important." Even though Lila's conceited remark would have made most people laugh, Sophia was too busy gazing at the beautiful sweater to do anything but smile.

"And now, if you don't mind a present that you can't open," Mrs. Wakefield announced, "we have some good news." Looking as if she could hardly bear to keep her secret a minute more, she begged Mrs. Rizzo to join her. Elizabeth's mother's eyes were dancing with excitement. "It seems that Mrs. Rizzo here is as talented as her daughter—in a different field. In Italy, she had her own shop, where she designed quilts and afghans."

Mrs. Rizzo smiled shyly. "But here, I—I have a problem with my English and with my—my legs." She dropped her eyes, but then raised them again, her face full of hope. "Mrs. Wakefield says her firm can use my pillows and rugs, that I can design for them at home."

"It's true," Elizabeth's mother told them. "In fact, I'll bet to develop a talent like this, my firm would even be willing to help finance an English course. It would certainly be a good investment in our future."

"And in ours, too." Mrs. Rizzo smiled broadly, her arms tight around Sophia. "When somebody believes in you, it is easy to do good, eh, Sophia?"

Sophia, still wearing her tiara, gazed fondly at Elizabeth. "You bet, Mama," she said. "When you've got a friend who cares about you, who encourages you and stands by you, you've got everything you need to succeed."

"Maybe that's true for all of us, Sophia." Mr. Wakefield pulled Elizabeth's friend aside to share a surprise of his own with her. "Your brother wasn't ready to face a crowd like this today, but while I was at your house, I gave him the name of a friend of mine. He's a psychologist who works with youngsters at the Valley Family Counseling Center." Mr.

Wakefield's smile was warm and reassuring. "He's helped a lot of confused children, and I think Tony would like him."

Sophia's happiness had been building, but now that Elizabeth's father had offered her hope that her brother might overcome his anger and frustration, the dam broke. Crying, she hugged Mr. Wakefield as if she would never let go. "Oh, thank you," she sobbed. "Thank you all for being such kind, wonderful people. Thank you for helping me and my mother and Tony. But most of all," she continued, as she grabbed Elizabeth's hand, "thank you for giving me the best friend I've ever had."

Minutes before, Elizabeth had been convinced that this party marked the worst moment of her life. Now, with Sophia's thanks ringing in her ears and her family and friends around her, she wondered if she had ever had a happier day.

The only thing that would have made it all perfect, of course, would have been to share the party with Jessica. But, as Elizabeth learned when her twin returned the next day, Jessica wouldn't have traded places for anything.

"I'm glad everything worked out for Sophia, Lizzie," she confided while she unpacked her three bulging suitcases. "But I wouldn't have missed *Shout* for all the birthday parties in the world!"

Jessica began to glide gracefully around her bedroom with an imaginary dance partner. "Oh, Terrence," she whispered, her eyes half closed, "being with you was positively the greatest experience of my life!" Then she opened her eyes and winked at her sister from across the room. "Terrence says he's sure Sophia's play was OK, but he and I know there's just nothing like singing and dancing!"

Elizabeth hated to spoil her sister's happy mood, but she decided she'd better fill Jessica in on what her father had told her after the party. "Dad wasn't so happy about the switch we pulled. He said we should both expect a punishment to suit the crime."

"What does *that* mean?" Jessica asked, stopping herself in the middle of a pirouette.

"I'm not sure," Elizabeth confessed. "He said he would take our good intentions into account, and that sometimes people break the rules for a good reason."

"Great, that means we're off the hook."

"Maybe not," Elizabeth cautioned. "You know Dad. He always means what he says. We did fool the Martins, and I did give Sophia's party without telling them."

"That's right!" Jessica stopped dancing and plopped onto her bed. "You broke twice as many rules as I did. So you should get the worst punishment. Fair's fair, Lizzie, right?" Suddenly, though, she looked stricken. "Oh, no! What if he grounds us?"

"If he does," Elizabeth admitted, "it won't be the first time."

"But he can't! He simply can't. It would spoil everything all over again!"

"What do you mean, Jess?" Elizabeth saw that her sister was genuinely upset.

"Didn't I tell you?" A smile replaced her frown as she remembered her good news. "Mr. Butler wants me to head the Mini-Olympics!"

"Oh, Jessica, that's wonderful!" Elizabeth exclaimed.

"Yeah! Provided Dad doesn't come down too hard, this year's Olympics are going to feature the biggest, toughest, best races ever!" She grinned at her sister, a mischievous twinkle in her eyes. "Why, blubbery old Lois Waller will be up to her fat ankles in sweat!"

"What do you mean?" Elizabeth asked suspiciously. "The Olympics aren't just for jocks, Jess. Everyone should have a fair chance to win."

"Not the way I see it, big sister. If people haven't taken the time to get in shape, then I don't think they should expect to win any prizes. And, for once, what I think goes. Don't forget. I'm in charge."

"I know it," Elizabeth told her, wondering what would happen when Jessica planned one of the most important events in the whole school year. "And I have a feeling that very soon, everyone else will, too!"

Will anyone have a fair chance to compete against Jessica? Find out in **ONE OF THE GANG,** *Sweet Valley Twins #10.*

SWEET VALLEY TWINS

Tell your kid sister, your sister's friends and your friends' sisters . . . Now they can all read about Jessica and Elizabeth in **SWEET VALLEY TWINS**—a brand new series written just for them.

You love reading about the Wakefield twins, and the whole gang at SWEET VALLEY HIGH. You love the real-life thrills and tender romance on every page of every SWEET VALLEY HIGH book. Now there's something new and exciting—it's Francine Pascal's latest series—SWEET VALLEY TWINS. These are the stories about Jessica and Elizabeth when they are just twelve years old, as all the Sweet Valley excitement begins.